Apalachicola
Mother of Pearl

Michael Kinnett

Published by:
Southern Yellow Pine (SYP) Publishing
4351 Natural Bridge Rd.
Tallahassee, FL 32305

www.syppublishing.com

This is a work of fiction. Names, characters, places, and events that occur either are the products of the author's imagination or are used fictitiously. Any resemblance to actual persons, places, or events is purely coincidental.

The contents and opinions expressed in this book do not necessarily reflect the views and opinions of Southern Yellow Pine Publishing, nor does the mention of brands or trade names constitute endorsement.

ISBN-10: 1-59616-081-0
ISBN-13: 978-1-59616-081-1
ISBN-13: ePub 978-1-59616-082-8
Library of Congress Control Number: 2019952935

Printed in the United States of America
First Edition
November 2019

Dedication

The city of Apalachicola, Florida, and the wonderful people who cherish and preserve its history.

Also by Michael Kinnett

The Pearl Series

Apalachicola Pearl 1
&
Apalachicola Gold 2

Apalachicola c.1880

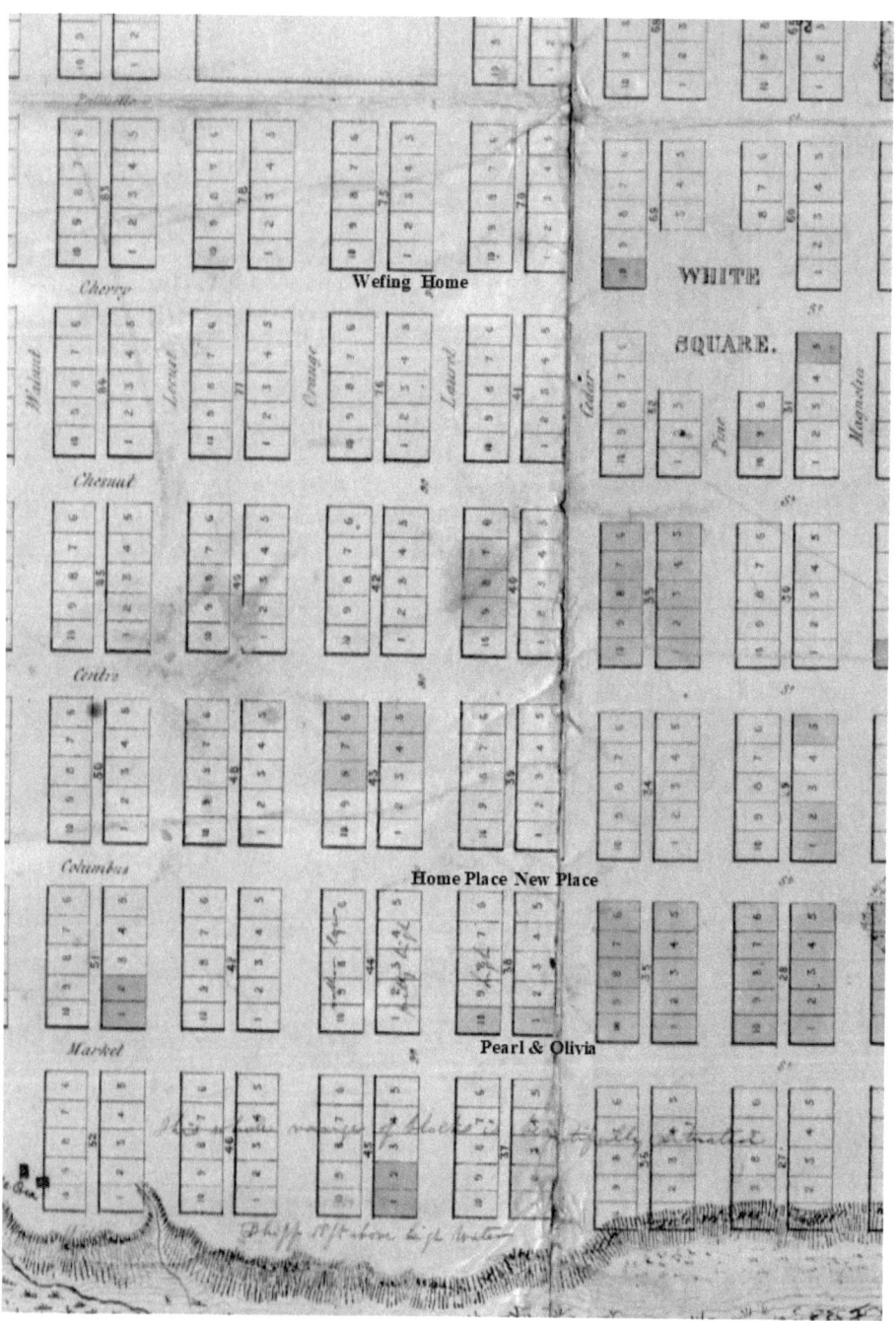

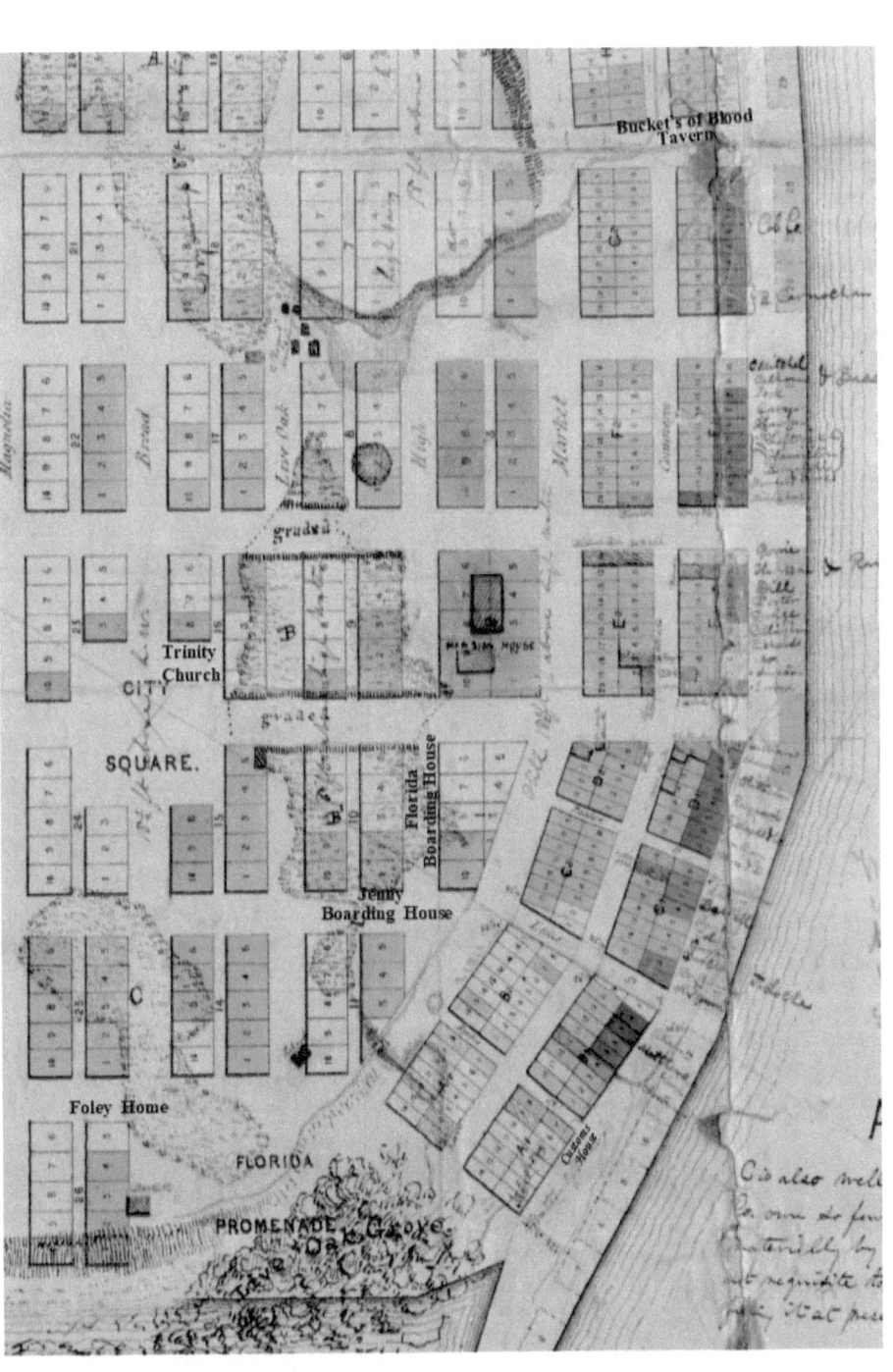

Preface

The stories of this family I've told up till now were from two journals I found while working in the attic of the Orman House Museum. I completed the first journal and presented it to you with the title, *Apalachicola Pearl*, the writings of Michael Brandon Kohler. The second journal I presented under the title, *Apalachicola Gold*, the writings of LaRaela Retsyo Agnusdei, known to most as Pearl.

The attic is now empty, but questions remain. What of Pearl's mother, and what was the terrible curse Airiana placed on her father, and did the evil remaining simply go away?

I am not a believer in things occult but may have, at times, led visitors to consider that I was; trying not to tread on their beliefs.

The next page of the story begins with a strange encounter.

Out in the country, I arrived unannounced at a most usual place, a private, landscaped garden in the middle of nowhere with an attendant at a gate. I was directed to a modest, well maintained, typical, country home where I was approached by a personal assistant asked if I had an appointment.

"No, ma'am. I just stopped hoping to find descendants of a family called Agnusdei."

"And what is your name?" she asked, looking at her tablet.

"Mike Kinnett," I replied.

"I have a Ranger, could that be you."

"Sometimes people call me Ranger Mike because I work in a state park, but it's not me; I didn't make an appointment," I explained.

But she didn't listen, announcing on her tablet, "Ranger Mike to see you." Turning to me, "Wait here; she'll be right with you."

Waiting quietly, it wasn't long before a young woman appeared, and with no words, just a reassuring smile, she placed an old book in my hands. "I believe this is what you're looking for; my mother is away on business so I'll have to do. Olivia Agnusdei Harris was my great-grandmother. Return the journal when you're through. All I ask in return is that our privacy remains intact, but I am certain I can rely on your discretion."

Confused I responded, "Of course," and the young woman turned and walked away. Please forgive me if I seem vague, but I consider this simple promise of anonymity a small price for answers to the questions plaguing my mind. It is because of this promise I cannot tell you her name or how I came to know of it.

It is from this strange encounter I now offer to you, *Apalachicola, Mother of Pearl*. These are the writings of Olivia Agnusdei Harris, the daughter of Pearl.

Michael Kinnett

Chapter I
In Harm's Way

I was six when my friends started bringing me their favorite books, asking me to read aloud. I can't remember a time when I couldn't read. My teachers called me distinctive, insisting I take classes with the older students, at first with their support and later to their chagrin when I won all the spelling bees. Grandmother Caroline said I got it from my mother who had taught herself to read. When it came to books, Mother went out of her way to keep me in good supply, but oddly enough, at times she insisted I put them down and go out with my friends, forbidding me from taking one along. My father was a teacher and a lover of words who made learning new words a daily game.

I remember being nestled in front of a cozy fire on cool January nights, taking turns reading from *Treasure Island*, *Twenty Thousand Leagues Under the Sea*, *The Three Musketeers*, and *David Copperfield*. I loved hearing my father read *Moby Dick* even though at the time I didn't understand the words, the passion in his voice held me spellbound. When I was ten, one of my short stories received rave reviews when it appeared in local papers, making Mamma and Gran very proud.

Gran started me working on a marking sampler at the age of five, embroidering my letters and numbers onto a fabric suitable for framing. I'm still working on my second sampler; it's pictorial, and Gran said it should reflect patience and skill as well as virtue, the value of education, and obedience to one's parents and to God. I scratched my head thinking, *a remarkable fabric indeed.* All I knew for certain was it had to have a steamboat.

***

Built by commerce in the middle of nowhere in a place a town should never have been, Apalachicola sits alone, surrounded by miles of water and nothingness. Always behind the times, we sit anxiously waiting as society trickles down a river or from across a vast sea. Departure is difficult; the roads are treacherous at best. I look forward to the day I'll live in a great city where the streets are paved in brick, and my calendar is filled with events.

Gazing over my shoulder, Mamma comments, "Being a little dramatic, aren't we?"

Staying in character, I continued dramatically narrating aloud. "Putting the back of my hand to my forehead, I turned to look upon Mother's face, professing yes... perhaps." Then breaking from my dramatic oration, I explained that after a brief pause I will finish the paragraph with, "I view it as my burden to record the drama of this place, and someday it will all be revealed in my novel. Mother, be advised, and choose your next words carefully knowing they may tip the scales as you precariously teeter on the cusp of being written as a villain instead of the heroine of my upcoming novel."

Mamma began to chuckle and looking to the heavens, she asked, "Oh, dear Lord, give me the strength to raise this child," and we both shared a good laugh.

"Finish up; company will be arriving soon, and you, being the guest of honor, need to be there to greet them."

"Let me finish one more paragraph, and I'll be down," I promised.

"Don't be too long. If you get carried away and forget to show up, I'll throw the food to the dogs."

Putting my writing tablet aside, I reached for my diary to make a more official record.

Apalachicola, Florida, January 12th, 1886, I Olivia Agnusdei Harris am celebrating my thirteenth year. My family and friends are gathering to join in the celebration—all but my father, of course, he having died of the consumption when I was seven. I'd like to believe, if not for the Grim Reaper, father would have been proud of me today. I often visit his marker at the Chestnut Cemetery. I sit by his stone, contemplating my life aloud and then imagine the rejoinder in his voice. I miss his counsel.

My Grandpa Kohler, one of the kindest men on God's earth, is beginning to show signs of decrepitude; at times his memories fade, and he may repeat the same stories every visit. Inflicted with bad dreams, he wakes screaming in the night. It is only in the presence of my mother, his little Pearl, he finds solace, and his mind becomes calm.

My mother is Pearl. She is my world, and I love her deeply, but I know, like my grandfather, she carries dark secrets.

As I closed my diary, Mother shouted up the stairs, "Olivia Harris, get down here…, now young lady."

"Yes, Mother, on the way." Running down the stairs, I made it to the door just as Gran arrived with my gift in hand. Although disappointed to hear Grandfather was too sick to attend with all the other guests, it was still a wonderful birthday.

***

The next morning, I was wholly engrossed in a wonderful gift I'd received from my mother, Mark Twain's *Adventures of Huckleberry Finn*, when she hollered from the parlor, "Olivia, where are you?"

"On the porch swing," I hollered back.

7

Pushing the screen door open with her elbow, she approached toting two, rather large, leather-bound volumes. Leaning over, she gently placed them on my lap. "You think your old Mamma might get you to put Huck Finn aside and do a little light reading?" I was about to tell her how I was at a very exciting juncture and ask if the journals might wait, but before I could speak, she said, "Lately you have been plagued with questions concerning family, and admittedly, I've been avoiding your questions. These journals hold many answers you seek. When you've finished, we'll have a long talk."

As she walked away, she hesitated, looking down and to the right, but not back. She gazed at the floor for a moment and in a trembling voice said, "I pray, knowing the truth, you will not think ill of your mother for the things I have done."

Suddenly, my adventure story paled in comparison to the journals I held in my lap. I immediately began reading.

As if possessed, I read, finding no rest for three days. Without a word, my mother brought me food, never once asking me to join the rest of the family at the table. Grandpa's journal revealed the series of events binding mother and him together. It never occurred to me my Grandpa Kohler was an author or could have felt so deep or grasped the world with such a profound understanding. I now see why my mother loved him unconditionally, for in the worst of times, he was there for her, and no matter his condition, she would be there for him.

Growing up, my mother never spoke of her family previous to her adoptive parents, Michael and Caroline Kohler. Of late, I had been asking questions about circumstances surrounding her birth and her natural mother, my grandmother Airiana. Up to now, the name Airiana was all I knew of my gran. The journals, belonging to mother and Grandpa Kohler, revealed the evil nature of my grandfather, Guillaume Gauthier Verheist. But with all I have discovered in the pages of these journals, I still know very little of the maternal family. It was in notations in the margins of her journal and small notes stuffed between pages where I found indications mother was even tenuously interested in her mother's side of the family. Both journals spoke of truth. I now find truth can be disturbing.

My Grandmother Airiana died shortly after giving birth to my mother. I never met my Great Aunt Etta, my grandmother's only sister. Etta passed away some twelve years ago, having died of an apparent suicide, although a note written in my mother's hand and an old newspaper clipping revealed a week passed before New Orleans' police were able to recover Etta's head for burial with the body. The family scuttlebutt led one to believe, Aida, Etta's oldest daughter, my mother's first cousin, simply disappeared from the face of the earth, but there was no official inquiry. A faded notation, I suspect an erasure, in a margin of mother's journal indicated her cousin Carina, Etta's youngest child, was still alive at the time of the entry; the notation was embellished with the words, "Smug little bitch."

When I finished, she came to me with a tear in her eyes and sat trying to justify her role in the death of so many. Until this moment, I questioned if some of what I read was fiction, but her reaction immediately convinced me of its truth. Even as a truth, I did not understand her distress, for no matter how evil she portrayed herself in these pages, the facts bore out my mother, Pearl, was the heroine of these stories. My mother felt Grandpa Kohler's journal was tainted, because love can be a blinding force, and he could find no fault in his little Pearl. Aside from facts only Mother knew, Grandpa recorded an accurate account.

In his journal, Grandpa Kohler compared history to the Apalachicola River, for just as the water of our river is connected to all the waters of the world, so does all of history share a connection. To find these histories, one must look beyond the family Bible to places where our pasts collided and touched the lives of others. It is in the writing of others that we gain true insight into our own legacies.

We spent countless hours poring over every sentence of both journals. I believe it did her a world of good reliving the past and knowing my reaction was not as she had feared. As we studied together, our relationship began to change; my mother began treating me more as an adult. Grandpa felt that I was too young, and mother should have waited, stating in no uncertain terms, "Preferably after I'm dead." At the time, Grandpa nor I knew mother held a secret. Still aloof about her mother's family, I once again started asking questions about my Grandmother Airiana. Without saying a word, mother reached in her apron pocket and handed me a calling card. Scribed on the front was the name Agnusdei and an address in New Orleans, but on the back was written, "Beware the ides of March," and it was signed with the initials, "C.A."

Confused, I asked, "What is this?"

"A few months back, I found it slid under the front door," she replied.

"Where is the envelope? Did it have a postmark?" I inquired.

"No, it was hand-delivered just as you hold it now," mother said.

Scrutinizing the card, I puzzled. "Rather cryptic, very Shakespearean; Julius Caesar is dead. Any idea who's in danger?"

Hesitating and reluctant to answer, she reached over and taking my hand responded, "You Olivia. I believe it refers to you."

Suddenly, with a knot the size of a fist in my stomach, I reacted. "What! I don't know these people. Why?"

"Because you are an Agnusdei woman and have come of age," Mother said, gripping my hand tighter.

Still in shock, I fired back, "Who sent this, who is this C.A.?"

"At this point, I can only venture a guess, but I'd say this note was sent by Carina. Why I cannot imagine. But I assure you I will find out. I am so sorry to put you through this; no thirteen-year-old should carry such a burden, but I thought it was best you knew just in case, heaven forbid, something should happen. You see why it was important you read the journals now instead of later."

A little frightened, I told her, "You're scaring me. What should I do? I have no clue."

With a quick response, "You—there is no you in this affair—you will do nothing. I will handle this. I've planned a trip to New Orleans and will be leaving Thursday. What you will do is stay with your Grandma and Grandpa Kohler and wait patiently for my return. Do you understand?"

"But, Mother," was all I could utter.

Before raising her voice, she reiterated, "Do you understand, Olivia Harris?"

"Yes, Mother," I relented, and although I said yes, in my mind, this was far from over.

The journals revealed what I suspected all along; my mother led an extraordinary life. It is hard telling what she may have achieved had her circumstance been different, but after a long think, it occurred to me that it was because of her circumstance she achieved great things; it couldn't have happened any other way.

Staring into the kitchen, I struggled to wrap my mind around the fact that the woman standing at the sink in her apron, washing dishes, possessed a treasure beyond imagining, and yet we lived a frugal life. Mother always said, "Wealth was a curse and a cross to bear."

At an age when I was being encouraged to excel in my schooling, this woman I called Mamma was picking up a knife and making impossible decisions, succeeding where all others failed. She loved others more than herself, finding happiness, not in gold but from all the beautiful little intangibles created in a loving family, intangibles most take for granted.

So many were in her debt, but she expected nothing in return. The very heart of a great movement, it was through her people that she found the courage to be extraordinary. Generations owe their freedom to my mother, yet the evidence of her passage remains hidden away in the pages of these journals and the silent testimony of the dead.

My mind was set. Tomorrow morning, I will be on the first steamer heading to New Orleans. My mother has paid her dues; it is time for me to step up and assume the mantle. I will not allow her to stand in harm's way for my benefit. I have one stop before introducing myself to the family. In her journal was a letter from one Matthew Rutledge stating he'd found the place of her birth. A crude drawing on the letter showed a line marked Mason Creek, a square identified as Central Hotel, and behind the hotel appeared a small X. Not much to go on, but I loved a challenge.

Hollering into the kitchen, I asked, "Since I'll be staying with Gran and Grandpa Kohler, anyway, maybe I should go tomorrow. I know

Grandmother Caroline would enjoy the company and give her a break from Grandpa's stories."

"What a wonderful and thoughtful idea, Olivia, spending time with your grandparents and helping them out. It'll give me a day to pack and prepare for the trip, and we can all get together for supper on Wednesday night before I leave," she replied.

Hopeful, with a slight whine in my voice and my very best hangdog look, I inquired, "Is there any chance you'll change your mind and let me tag along? I'd love to meet the family."

"Maybe next time sweetheart. It's best if I meet them first, and I resolve a few issues before they meet you. My heart is aching at the thought of us being parted. I will miss you terribly," Mother sighed. "You do remember what your Grandma Caroline says about absence don't you?" Then prompting me, she repeated, "Absence?" Then silent for a moment, she waited for the inevitable reply.

Rolling my eyes, in a sarcastic voice, I finished the quote, "I know, I know, 'makes the heart grow fonder,' but as far I'm concerned absence just makes me sad."

First thing in the morning, I was off like a shot, kissing her on the cheek, "Love you, Mamma. See you tomorrow for supper," and with bag in hand, I was out the door heading to Grandma and Grandpa Kohler's house. Grandpa was still sleeping, and Grandma was in the kitchen when I stole unseen into the house. Leaving a note on the dresser in my room, I exited through the window, heading to docks.

The ticket office was open, and to my good fortune, the man selling fares was new to town and didn't know me; a coastal packet was leaving in forty minutes. With time to kill and this being my first deception, I nervously headed down Water Street, trying to walk off the anxiety with guilt now possessing my soul.

While some in town were slow to rise, Apalachicola commerce was wide awake. Looking down toward the mouth of the river, the Kennedy Lumber Mill was up and running, its large conveyor carrying sawdust and scraps out to a barge where a perpetual fire burned. The fires from the lumber companies along Water Street made old residential areas uninhabitable thereby pushing the new construction down Market and Columbus Streets, creating new upper-class residential neighborhoods.

The death of the cotton trade and the Terrible War left Apalachicola in a state of ruin. Our salvation came in the 1870s when lumbermen realized it was easier to float logs down river than to push them upriver to the railheads at Eufaula or Columbus. Thanks to European financiers supporting foreign lumber trade, today the ledgers showed shipments to Europe comprise nearly half of all lumber shipped from our port and a quarter of all trade from the port of Apalachicola.

Only a handful of men and companies dominated Apalachicola's lumber industry, and with new partnerships forming every day, it was hard at any given time to tell who owned what. James Coombs had recently partnered with Charles Emlen from Pennsylvania, creating the Coombs & Emlen Company located on the wharf below Centre Street. They manufactured hewn logs for European and South American trade, but there was talk going around town that Emlen had plans to withdraw from the company and that Coombs was going to partner with a man out of Mobile named Seth Kimball; it was all very confusing.

Lumber was the biggest but not the only industry in town. Walk just a short distance up Chestnut from the Kennedy Lumber Mill, and you'd pass by the Grady & Co.'s store, Munroe & Co.'s office, the iron works, and McGlynn's furniture factory, just to name a few.

Jas. W. King,   Apalachicola, Fla.

The Bank and J. E. Grady & Company

Herman Ruge and his two sons, George and ill-tempered John, recently took over a not so successful canning plant down at the mouth of the river. Building on the knowledge of Chesapeake Bay canneries, the new Ruge Brothers Packing Company had developed a method of pasteurization they believed would revolutionize seafood canning and bring Apalachicola bay oysters to the world market, thus opening a new era in Apalachicola's seafood industry.

Ruge Brothers Packing Company, Apalachicola, Florida

Just past the cotton warehouses, Orman House came into view; perched upon its high bluff, the Orman House stood as a symbol of a glorious past. This was the home of my mother's dear friend, Miss Sarah Genevieve Orman, known to most as Miss Sadie. Sharing a surreptitious past and holding an intimate knowledge of one another, she and mother often held council. I supposed knowing anyone so well would either create unbreakable bonds or a mortal enemy. I am glad they chose friendship. Miss Sadie lived in the house with her father, William T.

Orman, her mother, Anna, and her grandmother and namesake, Sarah Genevieve Orman.

Orman House

Before the journals, I had no idea my history was so entwined with the Orman Family and Miss Charity, one of their thirty-five slaves. I moved down the street just far enough to see the roof of Miss Charity's slave shack. Miss Charity, a loving, nurturing, old slave woman was the first to see the divine grace flowing from a little girl called Pearl. She served as Pearl's guide, helping her find a higher purpose. I envisioned my mother, a young Pearl, retrieving a camphene lantern from the mule barn then crawling down into a darkened chamber and discovering a hidden treasure.

Before the journals, I thought of Apalachicola as a dreary, backwater, port town where nothing ever happened, a place where you grew up looking forward to the day you could leave, but I stand here today transformed, never to look upon this town the same again. I am guilty of living here my whole life but never really seeing.

I have passed this way a thousand times and never taken notice, but standing here today, looking across at the old Blood's Tavern building,

I can't help but envision Bella lying on a table with her throat slit, and mother standing in the street, covered in her friend's blood, screaming.

With tears filling my eyes, I noticed the Customs House at the far end of the street, imagining a strong, young Michael Brandon Kohler, my grandfather, being kidnapped by the Rebel Guard, held captive at the slaughterhouse, and then forced to watch as his best friend Stillman Smith suffered a fate so horrific words cannot describe.

Glancing upstream, I looked forward to the day when mother and I might travel up river and place our hands on Ponder's grave to thank him for his unconditional love. The sound of a boarding whistle snatched me from my daydream, and I hurried back to the dock.

The steamer was pulling out when I noticed the man speaking with the captain was my Uncle Hatch. Although not really related, more of an honorary title granted him by my mamma when she was little Pearl, I grew up calling him Uncle Hatch. Known to most as Captain Hatch Wefing, he was one of my family's oldest and dearest friends. Captain Hatch Wefing was a hero of the journals, and I'm sure if you were to listen to his account of events, he'd tell how he single-handedly saved the town from the Rebel Guard. Besides my mother, he is the last person I wanted to see. I quickly moved into the shadow of the lower deck to avoid detection; this was going to be a long trip. I was familiar with several passengers, but Uncle Hatch was the only one I knew for sure would tattle.

I found the breezeway running across the center of the lower deck to be a perfect place to hide from the prying eyes of nosy uncle. Located just ahead of the paddlewheels, it offered open access to both sides of the boat. Windows in the breezeway gave a view into the passenger's common area, and the common area was surrounded by windows offering a view to the scenery off the bow. From here, I could easily see Uncle Hatch approaching and exit in either direction. Filled with benches and tables, the common area was sparsely occupied, just a few passengers reading books or napping; nearest the breezeway door, a few men sat at two small tables playing cards. I was just settling on a bench when John Milliken Parker from Mississippi introduced himself at one of the tables and asked to join the game.

The talk at the tables never missed a beat as it flowed from one unrelated topic to the next covering weather, politics, the best peach pie in the south, and religion. It wasn't until they started talking about niggers and immigrants my stomach took a turn for the worse. "Your nigger problems pale in comparison to the Irish flooding into the country," one man said.

Another in agreement stated, "We gotta get a handle on these immigrants. They're going to be the downfall of this country if we don't act soon."

That's when John Milliken Parker spoke up, "The Negros and Irish have nothing on the Italians, just a little worse than the Negro, being if anything filthier in their habits, lawless, and treacherous."

Men raised their glasses and drank a toast to him. His words cut me deep; I never heard anyone talk so harshly about my heritage before. Did none of these men claim a family heritage outside the United States? In the future, I hoped people were smart enough to see through his lies and contempt and simply ignore him.

I decided, that to stay out of sight, it would be best to spend the night on a bench, tucked away in the back of the common area. Using my bag as a pillow I settled in for the night. I had little expectation of sleep for my mind was buzzing like a beehive.

At the end of my bench on the wall hung a picture, I had seen it earlier in the day and this was not the first time I'd looked upon the image. Some magazines like Harper's Weekly would publish popular artwork suitable for framing saying it was their way of bringing art to the public, they didn't fool me I knew it increased circulation. It was a picture of an oil painting by William G. Yorke and at upon first glance, was a magnificent seascape showing three ships traversing the wave. Mamma showed me the picture years earlier and believed it to be the most abhorrent of art. The small brass plate carried the name

The *Wanderer* was a topsail schooner 108' long with a 26' beam. Built in 1857, it was the fastest ship on the Atlantic able to make twenty knots in a favorable wind. It was soon modified from its original purpose and could now transport as many as six-hundred souls. The souls were purchased on September sixteenth, 1858, at the mouth of the Congo

River in Africa. The cost was fifty dollars a head but no gold or silver changed hands just the hard-barter goods of gunpowder, armaments, and rum. Three ingredients that could always assure the ignorance of men.

The import of slaves was banned by the Slave Importation Act of 1807, but it didn't seem to matter much to the owners of the Wanderer. Four hundred eighty-seven slaves, between the age of 13 and 18, were loaded into the holds of the Wanderer, but on arrival four hundred nine departed the ship. Those who survived were sent to the slave markets of Savannah and Augusta. A few were sold in the markets of South Carolina, and some were sent south to Florida.

Even when the authorities caught up with the slave traders, putting them on trial, there was little mention of the disparity in the numbers. Formally charged with slave-trading, a hanging offense, the crew was tried in a Savannah court summer of 1860 the trial held the attention of the nation, but the defendants had little trouble being acquitted in the southern court.

A closer examination of the painting reveals the ship in pursuit firing a shot from the port bow chaser attempting to stop and board the *Wanderer*. The rather large sharks depicted off her stern distracts the eye from the much smaller slaves struggling to stay afloat after having been thrown overboard. How many died before a panicked crew realized they'd easily escape with superior speed.

Uncle Hatch once told me a story that made the hair stand up on the back of my neck. It was his rendition of the Flying Dutchman, a ship crewed by the damned, many on board recruited by Yellow Jack himself. Yellow Jack, a character drawn to represent Yellow fever was portrayed as a skeletal figure in a sailor's uniform knocking on a door, it was not a door you wanted to open. Staring at the image I knew that in Uncle Hatch's story the name of the ship was all he had changed. If ever there was a ship crewed by the damned it was the *Wanderer*.

Gazing at the picture my heart wept for all slaves aboard, but I felt outraged over seventy-eight lost at sea. How could my Mamma, the little child Pearl have fought against such overwhelming odds when her accomplishments could be negated in the holds of one evil ship.

Making port just before sunrise, I woke feeling stiff and sore, having spent the night on the bench trying to stay out of sight. During the night, some kind soul took pity and threw a blanket over me, but I had no right to complain of the cold. Any hardship on this journey paled in comparison to the hardships little Pearl faced. I wasn't alone like Pearl; if confronted with danger, I knew all I'd have to do was scream, Uncle Hatch.

Sitting in the shadows waiting for my chance to disembark, I began thinking how foolish I'd been. I should have snuck in late and hid away in my sleeping berth.

Uncle Hatch took his time leaving and was engaging everyone in conversation. Tired of waiting, I watched him closely, and as soon as he crossed to the other side of the boat, I scurried off.

Chapter II
Mason Creek

A block away, I hailed a carriage.

"Where to Miss?" the driver asked.

"Central Hotel please," I requested.

"Which one Miss? We have two Central Hotels."

Referring to my map, "The one on Mason Creek please."

"Central Hotel on Mason Creek…. Miss, are you certain?" he questioned.

"Yes sir, if you please," I reassured him.

"I'm glad you knew to say Mason Creek 'cause I was wrong about there being two Central Hotels." Smiling he looked back and said, "It is your good fortune I am old and one of the few who knows the way to the third."

Shouting a command to the horses, they started down the road.

This was my first trip to New Orleans, and I looked forward to seeing some of the city sites on the carriage ride but was sorely disappointed; the dock was on the outskirts of town, and this Central Hotel seemed to be more rural, not what I expected, but it was a pleasant enough ride. We passed a few small, well-kept communities and a couple of plantation mansions, the like of which I had never seen. I was staring at one the mansions, and as we passed the driver remarked, "Best keep your mouth closed, Miss; you might swallow a bug."

Closing my mouth, I hollered up, "Good advice. I'll remember that in the future," and we both had a little chuckle.

The ride lasted about thirty-five minutes and ended abruptly when we pulled up to an old, rotted, falling-down sign. Through the chipped and faded paint, you could just make out the words, "Central Hotel, Welcome." The hotel was a burned-out hulk covered in vines.

Making conversation, my driver perked up, "Yep, hard to believe, but before there were trains, this was quite a showplace. The Yankees burned it during the Battle of New Orleans. The owner, he disappeared and never came back.

Central Hotel, back in the day.

"Young Miss, I hope you don't mind my sayin', but lookin' at your face, I don't think this is what you expected."

"No, not at all, but it is the right place. Where is the Mason Creek?" I asked.

He was puzzled at first but then responded with a smile, "Mason Creek ain't a river Miss; it's a man. This road used to be called Mason Creek 'cause old man Creek used to live just up the road, and he was a thirty-second degree Mason. At one time, he was well known in these parts for having built a Masonic Lodge next to his house. The house is long gone; the Yankees burned it, but some of them Yankees was also Masons, and they decided to spare the lodge building.

Now Miss, if you got questions need answered, you might consider walkin' down the road a piece and talkin' to the crotchety, old, black man what lives in the old lodge building. He's been here his whole life. Now, I don't mean to be scarin' you none 'cause they ain't no need to fear him. He's old and a little bitter, but he's got a heart of gold. Do you intend on stayin' here awhile, Miss?"

"Yes sir; any suggestions how I might get back to town?" I asked, with a slight hesitation in my voice.

"Tell you what Miss, I'll be back this way in about four hours, and if you still need a ride back to town, I will be happy to accommodate you," he nodded.

Relieved, I smiled, telling him, "You have been very kind, and I appreciate and accept your offer," nodding back an acceptance. I paid the fare, and he drove away down the Mason Creek Road.

My heart sank into my shoes when looking around, and it struck me; I was alone. It may have been a sunny, bright morning, but it didn't change the fact it was one unnerving old building. Just then, a chill ran up my backbone, causing me to feel a little faint. Talking aloud to myself I said, "Get a hold on yourself girl. It's a beautiful day. There's nothing threatening here except the cobweb floating around in your brain. Get on with it; come on, one foot in front of the other," and with that said, I cautiously headed toward the hotel.

I don't really know what I expected to find, perhaps a table filled with the answers to all my questions. In reality, I found exactly what one would expect to find in an old, burned out hotel—absolutely nothing but a home for raccoon and opossum. Looted many times over the years, anything of value had long since been removed. But when all was quiet, I could feel a presence, the essence of the Central Hotel still evoked memories of a glorious past. After a thorough search and much contemplation, I headed down the road to visit the Masonic Lodge.

As I turned off the road toward the lodge, a voice issued a warning, "Who dat? This be my home; they's somebody livin' here. Git and leave me alone. Go on 'bout yo' business 'cause you got no business here. Y'all need be movin' along down dat road."

"Sir, my name is Olivia Agnusdei Harris, sir. Please sir, would you allow me a question or two? It's about my mother."

A black man appeared at the window and called out through a broken pane, "Why you just a slip of a girl. Why you out here in da middle of nowheres pesterin' an old nigger for? Agnusdei be a strange name. Has we met before?" he asked.

"Not to my knowledge, sir," I responded with a smile.

"You alone girl? Ya' ain't got a bunch of robbers hid in the wood, does ya?"

"No sir, just me. I'd swear on a Bible I'm alone. The carriage driver who brought me said I should talk to you; he said no one knows this place better than you," I said, trying to assure him.

The door opened just a crack, and he gave me a good looking up and down. Then after a slight hesitation, he beckoned with his hand, "Well... I 'pose it be okay you come up on da porch, and we have a listen to them question you got." Setting himself on a chair, he waited for me to join him.

"What shall I call you, sir?" I asked.

"I ain't a slave no mo', so you bein' a small girl, I 'spect a little respect. You call me Mr. Ezekiel. Dat gonna be a problem fer you girl?" he glared.

"Sounds good to me, Mr. Ezekiel," and I held out my hand to shake. Old habits die hard in the south. Hesitating, he looked around to see that no one was watching. Only then did he take my hand, and we shook.

"Now... dat take care of me; would it be to your likin' if I should call you Miss Harris?" he asked.

"Yes, Mr. Ezekiel. That would be fine," I responded.

"Now... I gonna leave you for a minute, but you go ahead with one o' dem questions. I can heared y'all from the house. I's just thinkin' it might be more social of me if I'd slip in and get us some lemonade. Dat be okay by you, Miss Harris?" he questioned.

"It has been a long journey, and I am parched. A glass of lemonade would be welcomed, Mr. Ezekiel," I graciously acknowledged.

Walking back into the house, he encouraged me to continue, "Go 'head with you question. I's listen."

"The questions are about my mother. I believe she was born somewhere around here, maybe at the Central Hotel. As I spoke, in the background was the sound of clinking glasses, and Mr. Ezekiel on occasion repeated back what I was saying. "Yes Miss, ya say the Central Hotel."

"Lookin' for ya maw's birthplace?"

Backing out of the door, he carried a tray holding two glasses of lemonade. Being polite, I stopped my conversation, rising to assist by removing one of the glasses from the tray. Then again, just to be polite, I took a sip. Stunned by the flavor of this sweet nectar, I immediately remarked, "Oh my!"

Grinning from ear to ear, he looked over to me and very pleased with himself, he remarked, "Some say it da best lemonade in the south. What you say to dat, Miss Harris?"

"I'd say they are right Mr. Ezekiel, not only the South but North, East, and West as well," and for a long moment, we sat quietly sipping our lemonade.

"Do ya knowed the date when the birth take place?" he asked.

"Mamma never knew the exact day. She thought it somewhere around 1852 to 1854."

"What you mamma's name child?" he asked in a more serious tone.

"She was christened LaRaela Retsyo Agnusdei, her mamma called her Pearl. Her father was a man by the name of Guillaume Gauthier Verheist."

His reaction was profound. I was surprised when he didn't ask about Pearl being christened under her mamma's name. "I'm here because my mamma truly believes she remembers first light and her mother's face the day she was born. I have to say, I've always questioned the possibility a baby could have a memory so old. Information I've gleaned from our conversations, tidbits spoken but never written, leads me to believe an imagined memory rather than one actually lived. This may sound crazy, but she once told me she saw her mother's face surrounded by white

24

lights and hundreds of rainbows. Seemed to me to be a pretty fancy beginning for a childhood filled with so much need and tragedy."

Rising to his feet, he asked, "Will you walk with me, Miss Harris?" Extending his hand, he helped me to my feet. Following a half step behind, we headed toward the Central Hotel.

There was an impressive Live Oak in front of the hotel, and it was here we came to rest on a bench.

"Now…, let me tell ya, though I never learn to read nor write, I never felt myself the fool of no man."

"Of course not, Mr. Ezekiel," I said in agreement.

"I've done alright by me and mine. But I do, at times, wish I could put down on paper one of my stories. You think I might share a story with you, and someday you write it down so people might remember me?"

Pulling a pen and paper from my bag, I told him, "I would be pleased to do this for you, Mr. Ezekiel. How about we do it right now?" and I encouraged him to continue.

"When I've finished, I'll tell you what I know about dat question you ask me, but fer now, I'd like to share the tale of James and Ella."

I sat captivated as Mr. Ezekiel spun his tale. I wrote it down, and now as promised, for the record, I share my version of Mr. Ezekiel's story with you.

Pausing in her duties, Ella stood mesmerized gazing up through the crystal chandelier. White light passed through the crystals divided into a multitude of colors covering the lobby ceiling. Sweeping the porch, her husband James stopped, and leaning on his broom, he peered through the window, but he looked not at the chandelier but rather the reflection of the light in her eyes. No one could have fathomed the depth of the love he felt for this woman. As if trapped in time, the scenario played out each night as their master slept, and they cleaned and prepared the Central Hotel for the next day's business.

Master Paul always inspected and supervised the lowering and cleaning of the chandelier. It was the centerpiece of the hotel lobby, "imported all the way from Italy," he boasted to guests. It was no one's fault but his own when rusted screw heads released the cleat from the beam, and the rope feeding quickly through the ceiling pulley dropped the chandelier toward the lobby floor. Still tied to the rope, the cleat lodging in the pulley was the last chance of arresting the fall, but instead, traveling at great speed, the cleat hit the pulley ripping it from the ceiling. Shattering the quiet of early morning, everyone came running. Hotel guests opened their doors to see what all the commotion was about. Ella and James came running in the back door from the slave shack just as Master Paul appeared from behind the hotel desk.

"Oh, my Lord. No!" cried Master Paul as he moved around the hotel desk to examine the catastrophe. "What happened James?"

"I got no way o' knowin', Mr. Paul; me and Ella was asleep in bed. Just like you, I come runnin' 'cause o' the noise." James, worried he may be blamed, lowered his eyes, "Mr. Paul, you don't think James got nothin' to do with it fallin', does you, sir?"

"No, no, it ain't your fault. I'm just upset it fell at all. What time is it?" Mr. Paul asked.

"It be near half pass four o'clock sir," James responded.

"Sun's on the way; no need in goin' back to bed. You'd just have to get right back up. Ella, you just as well get the kitchen fired up for breakfast, and James you need to go fetch the cart and get this mess cleaned up," Master Paul ordered. Having received her orders, Ella headed to the kitchen.

Knowing his master's love of the chandelier, James inquired, "Mr. Paul, you want I be real careful cleanin' up all the pieces, and we try and fix it?

Shaking his head in frustrated despair, Master Paul conceded, "No James. Look at it. It's beyond repair. Look at all the broken crystals, and the frame is twisted; I'll have to try and order a new one."

"What you want I do with the all the parts n' pieces?" James asked.

Master Paul walked away rubbing his head in despair, hollered back, "I don't care. Consider it a gift. Do what you want. It's yours now."

As soon as Mr. Paul was out of sight, James smiled, and with a spring in his step, he headed to the shed to collect his tools. 'One man's trash be another man's treasure,' he whispered under his breath.

26

Soon returning, he did as ordered and removed all traces of the unfortunate happening. His cart now filled with glass prisms jingled and tinkled as it bumped down the path to the tool shed.

Over the next month, James spent countless hours preparing a surprise for Ella. One day, curious, she questioned him about his time away; inquiring she said, "James, you got you a woman hid out there in them woods?"

James, with his best reassuring smile, held her cheeks and kissing her on the forehead replied, "You knowed they ain't nothing out in them wood but a little creek and a bunch of old catfish. Woman, they ain't never goin' to be nobody ever come close to takin' your place in my heart."

Finally, the surprise was finished. James nearly burst having to wait three days until Ella and Master Paul left to do the marketing. Gently transporting his creation from the shed, he carefully mounted his own small version of the lobby chandelier on the ceiling above their bed, the lowest crystals hanging just four feet from the cotton stuffed mattress. As he worked, James imagined the sweet dreams Ella would have while falling asleep under all those rainbows.

Ella and Master Paul returned before noon, but James had to hold his zeal till all the duties for the Central Hotel were complete. By eleven o'clock, all was quiet, and James and Ella slipped away to the well pump behind their shack. Here, Ella drew a pan of water so she and James could clean up before bed. Always attentive, James took his time gently soaping Ella's back and shoulders, stopping as always to hold her tight and kiss her on the neck. Suddenly, James stopped and listened, "You heared dat Ella?"

"I don't hear nothin', James," Ella replied.

"Oh, I think it be one o' them old coons up in the ceilin' again. You best stay here whilst I have a look," said James.

Ella, worried, cautioned him. "Watch your step James; they've been reportin' the hydrophobee goin' around makin' animals go mad with the fever and foamin' at they mouths."

"Don't you worry none; only thing make me crazy is seeing you standin' there as God intended," and James gave Ella a good look up and down commenting, "Oh Lord, give me strength."

Ella wrapped herself in a sheet and scolded, "James this could be serious. You need to be careful."

James, with a candle in hand, slipped quietly into the shack, heading straight to the bedroom where he one by one began lighting the chandelier's whale oil lamps. With each lamp, the room became brighter and brighter. The light passing through the back and side window of the shack began illuminating the trees.

More curious than frightened, Ella began approaching the porch. "James, what's glowin' back there? You find that old coon? Is you alright James?" James remained silent as Ella passed through the front door and approached the bedroom.

The door opened slowly, and Ella's eyes lit up. James, taking Ella by the hand, laid her down on the bed. Then making his way around, he lay down beside her. Ella was dumbfounded, and I'll tell you the truth; if Ella thought anything ill of this gift, it would never be spoken because of the overwhelming love with which it was given.

Chapter III
Myth or Memory

When Mr. Ezekiel finished his tale, he took me by the hand and led me out back of the Central Hotel. Out of sight, hidden in the brush and vines, sat a rundown cabin. Entering through the front door, we passed through to the bedroom. Stopping at the doorway, he motioned me to enter. Dumbfounded, I could hardly believe my eyes. Pearl's memories were real, and here I stood, just outside of New Orleans, in a rundown, old, slave shack with a glass crystal in my hand. I began to cry, knowing I was standing in the birthplace of my mother.

Noticeably upset, Mr. Ezekiel, began to speak, "Miss Airiana, she a mighty purdy woman. I can't look to you now without I see her face.

Realizing I had not spoken her name, I asked, "How is it you know her name? I didn't tell you her name?"

"Here, Miss Harris…, look here at dis carvin' on da doorsill. What dat say?"

The carving was clear, "5 March 1852, LaRaela Retsyo Agnusdei born of Airiana."

Pointing to the side of the bed, he told me, "I stood right there and seen it all. I 'member it like it was yesterday," he told me, and he began to choke-up.

"Please don't stop," I pleaded. "Tell me all you know?"

"You grans, they come and was in a bad way. Miss Airiana, she done lost her water, and dat baby was a comin'. But I figure it be a good thing 'cause they was here and lots of people willin' to help. But you grandad, he say they need hid 'cause bad men followin' not far behind want them dead.

"'Master Paul,' he say to me, 'take them back to James and Ella's place and hide them away. Be sure to keep 'em quiet.' So I done just as he say. Well… them men, they show up, but Master Paul, he act like nothin' ever happen. He sent 'em on down the road chasin' they own tails.

"Miss Ella, she be attendin' to your gran, and I commenced to lightin' all the lamps in the chandelier so we got good light. But all the light show is Miss Airiana bein' in a bad way and bleedin' terrible. Miss Ella, bein' a midwife, seen this many time before, and she knowed they ain't much hope.

"As kind as Miss Airiana was, your grandad, he was an evil man, and Lord know he hate niggers. He screamin' at Miss Ella. He say, 'Kill dat baby, and save my woman.' And dat just what she was to him, his woman. He act like she more his slave dan a wife. Not long after, little Pearl come into the world, but he don't want nothin' to do with little Pearl.

"By dis time, Miss Airiana knowed she dyin', and she ask to write a letter. Now…, I toll you I can't read words, but I tell you, the signs she drawed on the paper ain't from dis world, and dat look she gave yo' grandad just 'bout turn him to stone. Huggin' little Pearl tight, she toll him, even when she dead and gone, if he don't care for her baby, she gonna bring the gates o' Hell down on his head, and the dead will rise to drag his sorry ass to Hell. It was a terrible curse she placed on him.

"When Miss Airiana pass away, yo' granddaddy storm out the shack and was just gone. Now…, Miss Ella, she barren, and holdin' little Pearl in her arms, she start get all broody. James, he see a look in her eye and knowed for dat time bein', he a papa now. Master Paul, bein' a good man, he let us care for baby girl, and not long after dat, Pearl, she kinda become a guest of the Central Hotel."

Mr. Ezekiel began walking but continued to talk. "I followed him out the back door into the yard where his memories, thick as fog, filled the air. As though in a trance, he walked over and placed his hands on one of two wooden grave markers.

"Near two year pass 'fore you grandad come back for his property. He rip our little Pearl from my Ella's arms."

Whispering to myself, "You're James."

He continued on, "And just like dat chandelier, my Ella's heart broke beyon' savin'. She ain't never the same after she lose little Pearl. I tell you, my Ella, she go on livin', carryin' the burden till one day dat broken heart, it finally claim her life.

"I ain't never been a church goin' Bible thumper. Dat be Miss Ella's task, but I tell you, in the twenty some year since she pass, I ain't missed a Sunday. I thought many a time of takin' my own life, but the Bible, it say man go to Hell for dat, and I knowed dat ain't where my Ella is, so I keep ploddin' along, one foot in front of da other, just a hopin' someday we be walkin' together down dem streets o' gold. Fer now, I just keep on livin', waitin' for God to take me." Grasping the marker, reliving the past, he wept inconsolably.

Standing with tears in my eyes, I raised a crystal to the light to look at the rainbows. A familiar reflection in the crystal caught my attention.

"Mamma, you mad at me?" I asked.

"No child. I'm not mad at you," she answered.

"How long you been standing there, Mamma?"

Mother lightly touched my shoulder as she passed by, saying, "Long enough." Mr. James Ezekiel was devastated, tears flowing down his cheeks; his hands tightly gripping the marker. Mamma gently placing her hands over his told him, "It is an honor to meet you, James. I am Pearl. Releasing his grip, he and mother embraced and began consoling one another.

***

After a long while, we made our way back around the Central Hotel where I found Captain Hatch Wefing sitting on the bench, visiting with my carriage driver. "Hello, Uncle Hatch."

"Hello, Miss Olivia," tipping his hat.

"How long have you known?" I questioned

"When you bought your ticket," he answered.

"Why didn't you stop me?"

"Well, I'll tell ya why. It's 'cause there is a frightening, and I do mean frightening amount of your mother in you, girl. I knew when I saw Pearl's look in your eyes, there was no stopping you. It'd be best just to try and keep you safe." Holding out his arms, he gave me a hug; then finishing his thought, he whispered, "And tell on you to your mother."

"Grandpa Kohler was right; you are flap-jawed," I whispered back.

***

We spent two days camping out on the floor of the old Masonic Lodge, visiting with Mr. James, reliving old times, and mending old wounds. Her memories of the Central Hotel, of James and Ella were scattered and few, but I still found it amazing she remembered at all.

The first question I asked Mr. Ezekiel, "Was she a good baby?"

"Pearl never cry 'ceptin' when she was hurt, and clever, she done everythin' long for them other babies. She just a few months old when she start callin' Miss Ella her ma'am. We figure dat 'cause she hear it round the hotel so much. You know what I mean? We always sayin', 'Yes ma'am, no ma'am. I fetch dat for you ma'am,' to da customers.

Ella or Master Paul always be yellin' out my name, so she end up callin' me—"

Mother interrupted whispering out, "Jams, you were Jams," as she reached deep in her memories.

"You 'membered, Pearl. See Miss Olivia, I toll you she always clever. They all call me James, but what come out from your mamma was Jams.

Now you tell me somethin'; does your mamma still likes runnin' round neked?"

"Naked," I exclaimed.

"Yep, da one thing your mamma hate worse dan beets was wearin' clothes, specially her napkins. Ella no more get her all fixed up fer the day than she be hidin' over in sum corner taken everythin' off.

"Master Paul, he always be a chasin' her round the lobby laughin', clappin' his hand and stampin' his feet; he tell her. 'I gonna get you. You get yer clothes on girl.' Pearl she be runnin' full out, hands over her head just a squealin' and laughin', thinkin' she getting' away with somethin'. Ma'am and Jams, we just standin' in the kitchen door laughin', watchin' all dat foolery. Little Pearl, she what make the Central Hotel a home."

For his kindness and loss, like so many before, Mr. James would be assured of comfort in his old age; his little Pearl made sure of that.

We had a nice visit with Mr. James although I felt a little uneasy, knowing the subject of my disobedience was still lurking in the shadows. Over the years, I've learned a mother's silence can be the worst punishment of all.

***

Boarding a carriage, Mother and I began a wondrous journey to New Orleans, traveling roads sheltered beneath canopies of trees. Magnificent live oaks graced the lanes of old family homes dating to the times when the French, Spanish, and British fought wars over who would rule the territory.

Immense plantations of rice, sugarcane, indigo, and cotton held vast areas of land under cultivation thereby, fueling the southern economy. Nurtured by the Mississippi River, the mammoth port of New Orleans exported seventy-five percent of the cotton shipped from the gulf coast.

Like a moth to the flame, I was drawn to the charm of the old French architecture. The sights and smells of this place were enchanting, filling my senses, holding me under a spell. I had traveled twice with mother to New York, and it was exhilarating, even with only modest accommodations, but checking into the New Orleans' St. Charles Hotel, I felt like a queen entering my palace, and I remember thinking, *I could get used to this.*

After an unforgettable meal in the grand dining room, including two of my favorites, Atchafalaya soup, and crawfish étouffée, we headed to our room. Settling in on a parlor couch in front of a warm and cozy fire, the silence was now deafening. Feeling Mother's distress and filled with apprehension, I suddenly blurted out, "Are you upset with me?"

33

She calmly responded, "I take it since 'I'm sorry,' was not at the beginning of your question, it indicates your resolve for this matter?" she inquired.

"I am very sorry if I've hurt you, but I feel no regret for trying to keep you from harm. This threat was made against me, and I need to be a part of the solution," I reasoned.

"No Olivia, I am worried for you and with you, but seeing your resolve in this matter, I am not upset. I am, however, amazed I've managed to keep the Agnusdei bottled up in you for thirteen years," she stated with a sigh, shaking her head.

"Then what is it… if not angry, why so silent?" I questioned.

Choosing her words carefully, as if not to scare me, she answered, "For being thirteen years old, you are smart and clever, but what your Grandfather Kohler wrote in his journal is true; 'with age comes wisdom.' You have learned so much, but you have much to learn. I know you've read the journals and have imagined events and places, but you have yet to stand in front of a man who would claim your life for a handful of coins. There are evils in this world beyond your current grasp. We are about to confront one of those evils, and I will be your guide, but you must promise—you must swear an oath to obey me."

"Yes, count on me. I'll do my part. I promise…, but if the danger is so great, why not just walk away?" I asked.

"Sometimes you find danger, and sometimes danger comes looking for you, and when evil is stalking, never cower in fear. Keep your wits about you; turn and fight. Do you understand what I am saying?"

"Yes, I understand, but can you tell me why? I've never done anything too evil, so why does it stalk me?" I puzzled.

Mother calming her voice answered, "Well… we don't know for sure that is the case, do we?"

"No, not really," I replied.

"Let's not jump to conclusions just yet. Tonight, I'd like to tell you some of what I know and some of what I think, and I need you to listen closely." Settling in, I was all ears.

"Back in the old countries, Italy and Sicily, thirteen families controlled the dark arts. There were more who claimed the arts but only

34

thirteen with the money and heritage to lend any credibility to the practice. Many an old woman cast an evil eye, and many found the need to seek protection from their gaze. These families found profit in the fear and offered protection from unseen forces, protection at a cost.

"For generations, families of the dark arts feuded, and over the centuries many died. In an attempt to stem the violence, in the 17th century, a truce was called, and a gathering took place. It was a meeting of serpents, but of the serpents gathered, the lesser of the evils was elected to keep the peace. And the least offensive member of the family Agnusdei, a young girl, was chosen as judge; upon her death, the title passed to her daughter and so on and so forth, eventually passing to me and you. Those gathered paid tribute and committed support in the form of great treasures so that the family Agnusdei would, in turn, pass judgment and adjudicate issues plaguing the great families. Because of the agreement, the century passed in relative peace.

"In 18th century Europe, the beliefs in dark arts began to wane, and now fewer in number, the great families began to evolve, some into legitimate businesses, but for others, without the evil eye, it became payment for protection from violence, perpetuated by the families themselves.

"It has always been in the nature of man to expand his territories, and so it became necessary for family Agnusdei to splinter, sending one of the Agnusdei daughters to a faraway land called New Orleans where she began adjudicating old family issues in a strange new world. She would have been your great-grandmother.

"It was here in New Orleans where African, Haitian, and the old-world beliefs collided in a revival of the dark arts. Combined and bastardized, they became more violent, and people once again started seeking protection from dark and sinister powers.

"Unlike my mother, I never believed in the Evil Eye, Hoodoo, or Voodoo, but I must also confess, at times, it seemed as though unseen forces, virtuous or evil, seemed to shield the family Agnusdei.

"From this day on, we must not only protect ourselves from the criminal side of the family but also from those who believe in the dark arts and would inflict harm to enforce their beliefs on those who question. I cannot emphasize enough the importance of our proceeding with great caution. The danger facing us comes from the Agnusdei family itself. Over the years, members of the family Agnusdei, corrupted by greed and a lust for power, attempted to alter the family's line of succession.

"It was Etta, your grandmother's only sister who attempted but failed to secretly kill your Grandmother Airiana and me, her unborn child. Etta, claiming her daughter Carina was stillborn, had lied and was holding Carina hidden away ready to assume my identity, replacing me in the line of succession. Forewarned of the assassination, Airiana escaped and made her way to the Central Hotel where she died giving me life. Much to Etta's chagrin, word reached the old families of an attempt on Airiana's life, and many stopped payment, unwilling to trust the judgment of Etta, the new self-appointed matriarch. I fear with the Agnusdei fortune dwindling, it is through you they may attempt to forcefully restore the balance of power.

"The journals only spoke of Etta's new plot, exploiting the greed of your Grandfather Guillaume Gauthier Verheist and their attempt to pull me back into the family. As true believers of the dark arts, it was your grandmother's curse holding Dray and Etta at bay as they waited for me to come of age when they would be forced to make a decision how best to profit."

Astounded, "I had no idea it went so deep. It is all so sorted. How did you come by all this?" I asked.

"Some of what I tell you I learned as a child listening to Dray and Etta through a grate in the upstairs floor. Some is from Aida who haunted my every waking hour, spewing her bile about my mother and trying to frighten me of the family. But what you may not be aware of is your mother has many eyes. I even have a couple looking out of the back of my head." Startling me, she suddenly raised her hand to the back of her head then slowly turning and lifting her hair, she yelled out, "Wanna see um'?"

Letting out a little scream, I cringed, and with my hands over my eyes, I called out, "No, I don't wanna see um!" And we both began laughing, but I knew by her face that she made the jest, attempting to relieve my tension and lighten the mood.

Taking my hand, she advised, "I have faced my death many times. Always remember, survivors are those who keep their wits when all around are losing theirs. I want you to repeat it back. It is very important you remember."

She began slowly, and I joined in, "Survivors are those who keep their wits when all around are losing theirs." I promised I'd remember.

"Tell you what. How about if before meeting the family, we spend a couple of days exploring New Orleans?"

Excited, I feigned a casual reply. "Well... to my notions, I can't see where a couple of days would matter all that much," and then I started grinning from ear to ear.

Chapter IV
Old Crone

After a wonderful breakfast of crepes and beignets, we passed through the doors of the St. Charles to begin our journey. Mother called to a boy, "Garcon, Garcon." Moving off to the side behind a brick column, she engaged a hotel steward in conversation concerning our destination. Pausing briefly, she asked if I'd hail a carriage. Standing on the street in front of the Charles in all my finery, I imagined myself being mistaken for aristocracy.

A carriage pulled up, and I started to signal the driver when I noticed it was a private carriage. On the side was a large monogrammed A inside the Agnusdei coat of arms. My heart was in my throat. I quickly glanced over to mother who was staying out of sight while miming the word Carina. Two women occupied the carriage; the one closest to me I assumed was Carina. The other dressed in black taffeta, her face obscured by a black veil, remained a mystery. I did not move as the carriage came to a halt, its wheels passing inches from my feet. Carina, scowling at me through the carriage window bellowed out, "What's your family girl?"

Remembering what my mother told me, I kept my wits. Calming myself, I hollered back, "Harris, ma'am."

"Tarnation girl. What's your mother's maiden name? Simple enough, I want your mother's maiden name. You understand the question now?"

There was spite in both her reply and demeanor as she attempted to upset and throw me off balance. It was obvious she controlled through intimidation. But knowing her name gave me the advantage, so I halted for a moment to avoid a quick reply. I would not let her bully me into a confrontation on the street.

"Now... Miss Carina, no need in getting all distraught here on the street. Wouldn't it be better to continue our conversation over tea in your parlor?"

Taken off guard in a defensive tone, she responded, "No it would not, insolent girl; can't expect me to have a stranger with no name in my parlor," she scowled back.

"Forgive me if I seem insolent, but although we have never met in person, we do share a long history, and for the time being, why don't you just call me Pearl?" Using my mother name to throw her off guard.

Upon hearing my mother's name aloud, I didn't think the pallor of her skin could be any paler, but I was wrong. Glaring from the carriage window, never altering her gaze, she reached out and with a cane in hand began rapping on the luggage rail. The driver immediately held out a calling card, rudely dropping it at my feet. He cracked the whip and drove away; the last thing I heard was Carina shrieking out, "Two o'clock." I knew she was watching, so I waited to retrieve the card until the carriage was out of sight.

As I was feeling very faint, Mother joined me, supporting me by the arm. "What a performance. Perfect! I couldn't have done better myself," she boasted.

Puzzled, I questioned. "Standing here in New Orleans, in a multitude of people, how is what just happened even possible?" I asked, searching for answers.

Deathly serious, mother responded. "You're an Agnusdei woman; you eventually get used to it."

Heading back to the room, mother immediately began writing letters. Between letters, she lay out her plan, preparing me for any eventuality. She rang the front desk, and the boy from out front soon arrived knocking at the door.

"Son, I need these delivered within the hour. It is crucial you complete the deliveries quickly and remain silent about your task. No one can know."

The young man placed the letters in a leather pouch. Mother, taking his hand, placed a twenty-dollar, gold, double eagle in his palm. Closing his finger around the coin, she held tight. The boy stared at mother as she instructed, "Do exactly as I say. If you complete the task and all goes well, the next time we meet, I'll give you two more coins. Do you understand?"

"Yes, ma'am, you can count on me, ma'am," and he ran down the hall.

"They must suspect. Won't they find us here?" I asked.

"We're moving; by the time they get here, the only trace will be the names I left at the front desk, Etta and Aida Agnusdei. Let them chase their own tails for a while," she smiled. She had thought of everything, down to the names recorded in the guest register.

In her journal, my mother once wrote, "Curiosity killed the cat, but satisfaction brought it back." I hope there is some truth in this simple proverb.

***

The address on the calling card led us to a three-story, brick, Creole townhouse in a place known as the French Quarter. Balconies extending out of the second and third floor were embellished with decorative iron rails. Two dormers sat perched atop a steeply pitched side-gabled roof. On either side were matching townhouses, but they appeared dark and vacant. Doors and windows up and down the street were open in hopes of catching even the slightest breeze with the exception of the Agnusdei home. My first impression was intimidating, hostile, and uninviting, much like the greeting I received on the street.

Stopping two blocks away, we went over our plan. Just shy of the house, I was to engage a passerby asking for directions or feign a tumble. A young lady in New Orleans was assured of assistance from a gentleman passing by, thus ensuring a witness to my presence at the house.

"Do not eat or drink," Mother commanded. "You have twenty minutes. If you do not appear in a window, I'm coming to get you."

Walking down the street, I began to worry over the decided lack of people. No people meant no witnesses, and I was instructed to turn around. Looking down the street to my left, I saw a policeman making his way toward me. Mother was waving me back, but I held up my hand to indicate a moment. "Officer, might I impose on you to walk with me a block to my aunt's house? On my last visit, I was pestered by a young ruffian. I know the chances of it happening again are slim, but—"

Interrupting me, the young officer held out his hand, and smiling, he told me, "Not another word, Miss. If my escort will ease your mind, I'm only too happy to assist."

The officer and I had a wonderful conversation as we walked and continued the conversation for an additional ten minutes in front of the house. Standing at the door, I waved goodbye and rang the bell. Mother was watching and had to have been impressed with my presence of mind.

The door opened, and an old man in a long, roll frock coat showed me in. As I handed him my calling card, he responded, "You are expected, Miss, please wait here, and I will announce your visit."

The dimly lit hall smelled of dust and damp with lamps adding just a hint of kerosene to the mix. I watched as smoke from a poorly trimmed wick added yet another layer of soot to the wall above the glass chimneys and thought to myself, *Douse the lamps, open the drapes, and let the sun in; throw these windows open, and let the breeze rid the house of this stale air,* but I fear even aloud my plea would have fallen on deaf ears.

Even in a state of neglect, the hall was quite impressive. Large, ancestral portraits hanging from the walls sanctioned the eyes of the past to peer down as a testimonial to a proud heritage. The most impressive portrait hung above a doorway at the end of the hall, and as intended, I found myself drawn to this painting.

My breath caught in my throat when on the tarnished gold plate, I read the name of my grandmother, Airiana Agnusdei.

Looking up to the large painting, my eyes strained, adjusting to the low light. Suddenly, a chill ran down my spine as I stood gazing at a portrait of myself. The image captured in paint, frozen in time, showed a young Airiana standing poised in front of this very house. I gazed upon her face in a state of disbelief as I slowly realized this was my grandmother's home. The resemblance I bore to my grandmother was uncanny. It is no wonder I caught their attention. To them, I must have appeared as a specter standing along the road.

I was running out of time when the old man finally returned. Having to wait was an eventuality we had not considered with my twenty minutes dwindling. I needed a window to signal and delay Mother's entry. Walking back toward the front of the hall, he slid open a door, offering me entry into a drawing room. Feigning interest in the décor, I slowly made my way to the street side of the room. Slightly parting one of the drapes, I casually peered outside.

"Young Miss, the lady of the house is very sensitive to light and requests the drapes remain closed," he scolded.

While focusing my attention on him, and with my hand to my elbow concealed from his view behind the drapery, I signaled halt. "I am sorry. Forgive me, but after visiting with her in the street, I'd never have guessed Miss Carina would suffer a sensitivity to the light?" I questioned. His reaction was one of being caught in a lie. Uttering only a, "Huff," in response, he departed the room.

As the door slid closed behind the old man, Miss Carina entered through a passage in the back of the room. Shrouded in darkness, to the right of the fireplace was a door. I failed to see this door when I entered the room. "Miss Pearl is it? Will you join me?" she sarcastically inquired. Still looking to the door, I'd swear I saw it move.

"Why yes. Of course, Miss Carina; it would be my pleasure." I responded.

Continuing to speak, "Please forgive me for earlier. My name is Olivia." As I turned away from the window, I parted the drape with my elbow, the light suddenly illuminating the back of the room.

"Confounded girl, close the curtain girl," she hollered. Before the curtain closed and darkness returned, I saw four fingers of a hand just below the knob, holding the door open, just a crack. It was now obvious someone in the next room was monitoring our conversation.

"I am so sorry, Miss Carina. I didn't mean to aggravate your sensitivity to the light. You have my sincere apology."

"Where did you hear that? I have no sensitivity to the light; it's just that sun makes the house heat up is all." She responded. "Cyrus..., Cyrus! Bring the tea; we haven't all day to wait," she bellowed. "Here with your mother, I presume. Where is your mother? Might she be joining us for tea?" she inquired.

"No, I am here of my own accord to visit family and make a few inquiries. Mother doesn't know I'm here," I stated.

"How independent and so young you are to undertake such a journey from a backwater sinkhole like Apalachicola to a modern city like New Orleans. I am impressed," she added.

The door slid open, and Cyrus entered pushing a tea cart. He stopped only briefly, closing the door behind before rattling across the floor to the table separating our chairs. In addition to tea and the accoutrement was a plate filled with tea cakes. With my senses heightened, I immediately took notice that one of the teacups was half full; it seemed strange. Cyrus picked up the cup containing what appeared to be tea and filled the remainder of the cup from the pot. As he offered it to me, I held the cup, waiting as he poured and handed Miss Carina her cup. "That will be all, Cyrus," Carina commanded.

Nervously looking around, Miss Carina inquired, "Staying at the Charles, are we?"

"No, Ma'am," I replied.

"Don't you worry traveling alone? You might get lost navigating these streets?" she asked. Carina appeared very distracted, constantly looked around the room. It seemed as though the actions of her body moved contrary to her words. She gave the appearance of someone who was touched and by no means in her right mind.

At this point, slightly confused myself, I answered her question, "Oh no, not at all. I have a young friend who works on the police force here in New Orleans; as a matter of fact, he escorted me here today. He'll be picking me up later," I informed her.

Acting as if she didn't even hear me and without warning, Miss Carina leaned forward, and without even looking at me, she knocked the cup from my hand, exclaiming, "You clumsy girl. Look what you've done. The cup is irreplaceable, a part of a set our family brought from Italy."

Completely confused, I glared at Carina, trying to make sense of her actions. Still in an agitated state, looking around the room, she abruptly stated, "Well, not to worry yourself. I suppose it was an accident after all; let me pour you another cup. I mean, after all is said and done, one less teacup isn't the end of the world." And with that said, she poured me another cup from the pot, but before handing it to me, she took a sip. Then, retrieving a tea cake from the dish, she took a small bite before handing it to me.

"Here, try the tea cakes. They are delicious." I asked myself, *Could it be possible she is showing me the tea and cakes are now safe?*

Slowly, I began to understand her ruse, and following her lead, I responded, "I am so sorry about the cup. I can make no excuses for my clumsiness. It is my cross to bear." Taking a bite of the tea cake, I commented, "Oh, this tea cake is lovely, and thank you again for being so gracious over the broken cup. I feel absolutely terrible."

"So, Miss Olivia, to what do we owe the honor of your visit?" she asked.

"Simply wishing to connect with my mother's family," I replied.

"I'd imagine you have it in mind to leave with a few small tokens, possessions of your Grandmother Airiana, things you can take back to Apalach as a remembrance?"

Slightly offended at her tone, I fired back, "Not at all. I can't imagine you have anything I would want to possess, and the bitterness I feel here today is not an intangible I care to return home with."

"So, what about you? Do you possess any heirlooms of your Grandmother Airiana?" she inquired.

"My grandmother died giving birth to my mother; what leads you to believe there was an inheritance?" I asked.

"It is well known that your mother is not without means. The question is not out of line. So either Guillaume was a better provider than

44

anyone thought possible, or perhaps he or Airiana took a few of the family belongings with them when they ran off together," she scowled. She was making no sense; were her questions directed at me or for the benefit of the phantom seated behind the door?

I informed her, "My mother is self-made and has always been capable of taking care of herself. Perhaps your mother Etta or your sister Aida can shed light on the subject of my mother's worth, Miss Carina," I said, in an offensive voice.

Disillusioned, she calmed her voice, "Forgive me, child. I have misjudged you…. You don't know of the key, do you?"

Standing boldly, "Key, what key? I am leaving." Sliding the door open, I entered the hall, but as I reached for the latch, Carina, forcing me against the door slipped a note behind my waist belt then quickly backed away. I flung open the door for a hasty retreat.

Mother was standing on the walkway in front of the house, and I took my place at her side. Defiant in her stance, she pointed a heavy walking stick directly at Carina, stopping her dead in her tracks.

"Witch!" Carina screamed out.

Mother, thrusting the stick forward yelled out, "Bitch!" But the stick and my mother's gaze were not focused on Carina; instead, she looked to an upstairs window. Again, thrusting the stick forward, she yelled out, "Bitch!"

Withdrawing, we headed down the walkway toward the street.

Carina began screaming from the steps, frantically pointing at the walkway where my mother had stood. Hidden beneath mother's skirt on the walkway, she had made a rendering of the same evil sign she drew as a child on their bedroom floor. The same sign cursing their house then now cursed the Agnusdei home once again.

On either side, men exiting the doors of the vacant townhouses quickly made their way down the walkways, herding us toward the alley across the street. My heart was pounding out of my chest as we were forced into this narrow passage leading to what appeared to be a dead end. A few old wooden steps at the end of the alley gave access to the building on the right. We passed through the door just as the four ruffians entered the alley.

It was a hall lined with rooms. As we passed the first door, a large, black man blocking the doorway calmly said, "Afternoon Miss Pearl. Does my heart good to see ya, ma'am."

At the next door, "My daddy sends his regards Miss Pearl."

Room after room, men were standing, tipping their hats, and paying tribute to my mother as she passed. Turning briefly, she spoke, "You men be careful. I couldn't live with myself if any of you gets hurt."

The man holding the door at the end of the hall told my mother in passing, "You just go on outa here, Miss Pearl. We all just glad we could be here for ya; we got your back."

We exited the building onto a side street, but she started walking back around to the front.

"What are you doing, Mother? Can't we just leave?" I pleaded.

Taking me by the shoulders, she scolded, "You must trust me, Olivia. This has gone on long enough, and if we are to find peace in our lives, we must reclaim our heritage. Violence is all they know, and this is a simple show of force to establish our territory," she assured me.

Carina was standing in the doorway, and Cyrus was on his hands and knees scrubbing the sign from the walkway. The curtain in the upstairs window parted slightly as we approached, and when all eyes were upon us, we casually boarded a waiting carriage and departed.

Chapter V
Key

Appearing disheartened, Miss Carina followed me with her eyes as our carriage pulled away. Beleaguered, she struggled to raise a hankie waist high. Then as if resigned to her fate, her hand fell back to her side, and the hankie drifted to the ground. Why, when I had every reason to fear and distrust was I feeling empathy for Carina? Then I remembered the note.

With mother looking on, I began unfolding the paper so we might view its contents. Once again, my heart went out to Carina. The paper was folded as if by a child with many creases and no uniform shape. The creases stained with ink lead to a blot that nearly obscured one of the words on the page. I felt the wadded and ink-stained paper to be a reflection of Carina's state of mind.

Pearl:

You are well advised to flee; leave us to perish in the cesspool we have created. Forgive me, for a horrendous life has taken its toll and left me ill-equipped to live among decent folk. I can no longer distinguish friend from foe.

Insanity now dwells in the House Agnusdei. She is mad beyond all reason and will stop at nothing to recover the key. If you possess the key, then wait no longer and claim your birthright. If you are truly ignorant of the key and it has been lost to time, I implore you to leave this place and defend your homeland until all here have perished. I pray your God will look favorably upon the warning I offer and may see fit to grant me sanctuary from the ethereal plain.

Carina Agnusdei
Banca Monte dei Paschi di Siena

"Key, what key?" Mother asked.

"I don't know. She brought it up in conversation, wanting to know if Airiana or Dray left you an inheritance and was there a key?" I reported.

Shaking her head, mother reasoned, "Any inheritance, including a key, would have burned on the Albany with Dray and his men. I'm afraid it may well be the key is lost to time."

Pointing to the letter, I questioned, "What are these words at the bottom, Banca Monte dei Paschi di Siena?"

"A very old bank in Italy," she replied.

The road snaked its way north into the swamps but in a few short runs ran true enough, allowing me to see a shadow following in the distance. I alerted mother to the presence of a second carriage. She informed me there were, in fact, two, and they followed to assure a safe arrival. Had I spoken quickly, the question would have been, who are you, and what have you done with my mother? But I hesitated, and mother announced, "We're here."

The carriage turned on to a lane then passed through a gate where two armed men stood watch. Buildings and equipment lined the lane on both sides. I had seen an operation like this before. Cypress mills were common near rivers and swamps. Farther down the lane, a long wooden bridge carried us safely over a swamp. Not far past the bridge, with the mill just out of earshot, sat a most impressive home.

Mother wasted no time climbing out of the carriage to stretch and work out the kinks. The staff was waiting and immediately began carrying our luggage into the house. Worried about introductions, I asked, "Who are these people? Are they kin?"

"No…, this is our home," she smiled, heading for the house. She was taunting me. I saw it in her face. I heard it in her voice. She was definitely taunting me.

The question plaguing my mind had not changed, so I yelled out after her, "Who are you, and what have you done with my mother?" Without breaking stride, she continued on as if she hadn't heard me; her antics made me smile. For the time being, all I could do was hold my tongue and hurry to catch up.

By the time I passed through the front door, Mother was throwing open the French doors on the back of the house. The interior of the house reflected its commerce; cypress and hardwoods embellished the floors and walls in a most impressive display, and the furniture reflected a mix of many cultures with some pieces so ornately carved you lost track of their function and viewed them as art. I followed her onto a piazza, and it was here, with my mouth gaping open, I looked upon a second ocean.

"Lake Pontchartrain…, beautiful isn't it?" she asked.

Holding out my arms, I asked, "This is yours?"

"No, not really. It's ours," she smiled.

"When have you ever found the time to come here?" I asked.

"Just like you, this is my first time."

Spellbound we both just stood, trying to take it all in. We couldn't have planned this any better. Mid-January, what a perfect time to arrive. The evening air was cool; the mosquitos and biting flies were almost nonexistent. I had a hundred questions rattling around in my head, but with the sun low in the sky, I held them at bay. Holding Mother's hand, we simply enjoyed the evening, letting the trials of the day slip away.

After a thorough washing up with the luxury of hot water, we sat down to a lovely meal. Then with blankets over our shoulders, we returned to the piazza to warm ourselves by a small fire to wind down before bed. "Mother," I asked, "what is this place you own but never visited."

"Remember in my journal, I spoke of the Vicar and how he purchased land and businesses to use as staging areas to move the slaves to freedom. This Cypress mill was our westernmost bastion of freedom."

Curious, I asked, "Why have you kept this place all these years?"

"I was eight years old in sixty-one when the country declared war on itself. At the onset, both sides readied themselves to boast a swift victory, but before the end in sixty-five, two of every ten in our nation were dead.

Me..., I was a kid raised in wartime; massive casualties did not distract from celebrating victories." Thoughtfully, in almost a whisper, she contemplated, "I wondered if standing before the throne of God, a general would defend his actions using the words, 'acceptable level of carnage'. Even with death all around, I never considered it could happen to me. I knew to survive I had to make good decisions and grow up fast because my world didn't seem to care if I lived or died.

"Deep inside, I knew I had a purpose; there was a reason God sat me down in such a terrible time. I am indebted to so many: Miss Charity, Ponder, the Vicar, and your Grandpa and Grandma Kohler."

She stopped for a moment to wipe tears from her eyes. These were names she could not speak without crying. Finding her composure, she continued, "These are the people who elevated me and helped me to discover my purpose.

"With the end of the war in sight and slavery in its death throes, I felt we'd won, but I was naïve. The hearts of men were not changed. Unwilling to sacrifice their profits, commerce north and south simply found another way.

"After the War and the bullet passed through Mr. Lincoln's head, the drunkard Andrew Johnson came to power, and the cause of freedom so many fought for was set back by decades with the new President's black codes and laws. 'This is a country for white men, and by God, as long as I am President, it shall be a government for white men,' he wrote in 1866.

"The devastation of war on the Southern economy spelled opportunity for Northern businessmen who wasted no time picking at the carcasses of Southern industries, buying our lands and businesses for pennies on the dollar. The remaining Southern aristocracy and the commerce vultures from the North, once again, searched for a way to increase profits through the exploitation of black laborers. It became a matter of semantics as one man's slave became another man's prisoner. Convict leasing and peonage became the new slavery.

"Before the war, slaves had value and were capital investments. After the war, those same slaves, once thought of as hard-working and loyal, had found their freedom but were now labeled as a people of sloth and deceit. Freed slaves were willing to work long and hard for their own little piece of America, but instead they found themselves arrested by corrupt law enforcement on trumped-up charges like vagrancy, fined unreasonable amounts, which they could never hope to pay, then leased out of jails by local judges to coal mines, lumber, and turpentine camps. No longer a capital investment, they were enslaved as prisoners and leased for as little as ten dollars a month.

"With no hope of paying their fines, there would be no release. The companies were not held responsible for their wellbeing; they worked them six days a week. When they died, they were buried on company land in unmarked graves, and the company simply leased another black man out of prison.

"The old battle I waged against slavery pales in comparison to the new battle against this more organized and sophisticated form of slavery. The men you see in this camp, their fines have been paid. Today our cause is given voice by men of good conscience in the great halls of power, both state and federal. They work soliciting against the evils of peonage and convict leasing."

Passionately, she told me, "When we return home, I will add to my journal an entry expressing my hope that my daughter, Olivia, might someday take up the cause and carry it into the future."

Stopping abruptly, feeling she'd gone too far, Mother attempted to discount her own words. "Forgive me; you are too young to be burdened with your mother's old cause. I had no childhood, and here I am like a thief pilfering yours."

Deeply touched and slightly insulted, I told her, "I am thirteen years old and your daughter. Do you really believe over the years with people traveling hundreds of miles to pay tribute to your purpose, thanking you for their very freedom, I would not take notice?

"I have peacefully basked in your shadow long enough. Do you really not know how proud and honored I would be to carry on your stead?" Getting a little too weepy for our own good, I added, "Besides, you're near thirty-five years old, practically ancient. I mean, how much longer could you have?" Mother's mouth dropped open, and she pretended to strangle me for making the comment, but it was destined to end in a teary embrace.

Regaining our composure, I excitedly asked, "What's next?"

"Bed," she replied.

Wide awake, my mind buzzing like a beehive, I could not imagine sleep, but finding myself engulfed by a down filled feather bed, I was proven wrong.

***

We stayed to the end of the month at what I quickly ascertained to be the *Pearl Cypress Mill* much to my embarrassment having missed the large sign over the gate as we entered. My days were filled with housework as mother determined it would, "Keep you grounded." But in the background, I watched as she prepared for battle, keeping me at arm's length until a plan was in place.

Our evenings were spent at small functions where I was introduced to very diverse gatherings of fascinating peoples, but I must admit, the night's Mother and I spent on Lake Pontchartrain in a small, steam-powered skiff were my favorites. As Grandpa Kohler taught her, she now showed me basic navigation skills and allowed me to pilot the skiff.

Chapter VI
"Malocchio"

It was through back channels, Cyrus, Miss Carina's servant, that contact was made and a meeting was set. The multifarious conditions of the meeting convinced mother of Carina's sincerity.

The meeting would take place behind the Agnusdei townhousewhere an offset fence offered privacy and access between the back garden and alley. For two hours each day, Miss Carina was allowed to tend her garden. The roses lining the fence were her favorites, and the most labor intensive to maintain. Sheltered in the offset between the two fences, one could remain hidden from the house and from one direction down the alley. This space between the two fences is where Cyrus, instructed us to sit and the conversation would occur as Miss Carina, with her back to the house, tended her roses. I was now convinced Miss Carina was no more than a prisoner controlled by the shadowy presence in the window. With all eventuality taken into consideration, ensuring our safety, the meeting was set for one o'clock.

I was anxiously awaited the meeting as I peered out the upstairs window of the mill house, checking on mother's whereabouts. From this vantage point, I commanded a good view down the lane and could see Mother talking with some of the men just past the bridge. Suddenly, with a look of terror on her face, she began running toward the bridge. That's when all Hell broke loose, and the bridge exploded.

I screamed from the window, horrified as the force of the explosion lifted her, throwing her back on to the ground. Smoke and debris filled the air as sections of the bridge fell plunging into the water. Stunned by the blast but not deterred, she staggered forward throwing herself into the swamp, and she began fighting her way across to the house. Some men plunged in behind her while others ran down the shore to the boats.

Confused, I thought, *What just happened? Bridges don't just explode.* Little could I have known, Mother had just received word a Sicilian killer known as "Malocchio," one of New Orleans' finest, had been contracted to hunt us down. I ran to the stairs making it to the first landing when I saw a man kicking in the French doors. I knew I'd never make it to the front door, so turning, I ran back upstairs. In hopes of confusing the intruder, I threw the latches, locked, and closed all the upstairs' doors, hiding instead in a small dumbwaiter.

I heard the door frames shatter as the French doors gave way. The intruder wasted no time quickly entering, he ran up the stairs after me. Overwhelmed with a feeling of impending doom, I realized there was nowhere to go. Trapped, it was only a matter of time before he found me. I'd have been better off leaping from the roof and hoping for the best. One by one, the upstairs' doors were kicked open as the killer searched for his quarry. *Should I throw open the door and make a run for it or hope against all hope help would arrive in time?* Discovering the rooms were empty, he became deathly still. In my darkness, I'd swear I felt the moment his gaze fixated on the dumbwaiter door.

Then there was a gunshot—a dull thud, the shuffling of feet, and an agonizing moan, just before a heavy object smashed against the dumbwaiter door. Slowly it slid down the wall to the floor. Petrified, I sat waiting for a sign. Suddenly, coming to my senses, I screamed out, "Mamma!" Throwing up the door, I jumped out feet first and stumbled over a dead body, falling face down into a pool of his blood. Startled, I frantically struggled to my feet. Shaking violently, I stood staring at a body. The blade protruding from the man's throat had a handle of scrimshawed ivory, and on his forehead was the curious shape of a three-leaf clover.

Voices outside drew me back to the window. Covered in muck, Mamma lay still on the ground just shy of the front door; beside her lay a large, dead, cottonmouth moccasin. A stout man in a gray coat, wearing a confederate hat, approached from the house, gently picking her up in his arms. Jacob Foley carried his Pearl into the house. Running down the stairs, I assisted Jacob in placing her on a couch.

Without hesitation, holding tight to Mother's left hand, Jacob took a small knife and opened the wounds; then sucking out the poison, he spit it on the floor. Without releasing her hand, he removed a cartridge from his pocket. Securing the bullet between his teeth, he twisted the cartridge, pulling the lead free. Then after sprinkling a little powder in each of the wounds, he lit them on fire. I was about to pass out when Uncle Jacob grabbed me. Holding me up by the shoulders, he whispered, "Olivia, she's going to be alright. You're going to be alright. I need you to listen to me; be strong. Talk to your mamma, and let her know you're safe."

I took my place at her side assuring her we were going to be fine.

When I finally came to my senses, I noticed the arm of Jacob's coat was saturated with blood. The dark hole in the fabric was from the shot I heard. "Uncle Jacob, you're bleeding; you've been shot," and I pointed to the wound.

"No need to worry, Miss Olivia. It went through the meat. Didn't even touch the bone. I'll take a few stitches, and I'll be good as new," he assured me.

Unconvinced it was nothing, I got a little bossy and yelled out, "You men quit standing around. Get his coat off, and stitch him up."

Coming to, Mamma let out a little chuckle. Uncle Jacob looked at Mother and stated in no uncertain terms, "Yep, she's gettin' the hang of it now. Gonna be a regular chip off the old block. Bossy just like her mother."

The men began tending to Uncle Jacob's wound. As they worked, I overheard him order them, "Take that worthless carcass upstairs, quarter it, and throw it in the gator hole... except the head. I want the head." He was in a real mood for having let himself get shot, so I didn't dare ask, but I wondered why.

A couple of hours passed before the doctor arrived. It turns out, people generally don't die from the venom but from the infection and tissue death caused by the bite. On her left hand, the two fingers opposite her thumb had to be amputated to save her life.

Late that night, unable to sleep, I joined my Uncle Jacob down by the fire. I had no intention of crying in front of him, but after seeing him, I teared up all the same. I hugged him and whispered, "In case you didn't know, on behalf of the South, Grandpa Kohler, Mother, and me, thank you for being extraordinary."

Even Uncle Jacob started tearing up. After a long moment, he reached in his pocket and handed me a shiny, gold horn dangling from a chain. Examining the ornament, I asked, "What is it?"

"It's called a Cornicello. Over here, it's known as the Italian horn. I'm Irish, so it doesn't mean much to me, but in Italy, the horn will protect you from Malocchio, the evil eye. If I had given it to you sooner I may not have gotten shot.

Steadfast and integrity were the words Grandpa used to describe his friend Jacob Foley. Even though I knew he wasn't an uncle by blood, I felt pride in the fact that he was willing to freely accept the mantle and be my uncle. Uncle Jacob only ever talked about the war with Grandpa and those who had shared in the carnage. It was not hard to tell those who had served; the war had made them brothers, and when they embraced, it was in remembrance of those lost and a way to ease the pain of unbearable memories.

"You know something, Pearl, your Grandpa was right all along. Oh! I'm sorry Olivia, sorry it's that you just reminded me so much of your mother."

"That's okay, Uncle Jacob. What about Grandpa?"

"We used to argue about the war and the justification for war. Your Grandpa was always the smartest of three us; you know who I'm talking about: Me, Hatch, and your Grandad. I never understood why he wanted to hang around Irish trash like me or a loud, irritating, know-it-all like your Uncle Hatch." I noticed when he mentioned Uncle Hatch that although he was shaking his head in disapproval, his eyes lit up. I think it was his way of smiling.

"Your Grandpa believed," 'That the issues, as presented, were not as cut and dried as the politicians let on. In this war, there was no right or wrong, no clear black or white, just many shades of gray'."

"I, of course, argued, 'You don't have to be a theologian to have religious faith, and you don't have to understand all the reasons for the war. Just have faith in the leadership.' But your Grandpa was more learned that I, and this was a faith he did not possess.

"There was no minimum age to enlist, but you had to be thirty-five or under. Much to Michael's disapproval, I lied about my age, claiming I was thirty-four although I was nearer thirty-eight. Turns out, it didn't really matter, officials either believed me or didn't care. As the war progressed, and the body count increased, the only requirement became a warm body."

"Tell me about the war, Uncle Jacob."

"No, Olivia, I wouldn't do that to you, except to say you will never have a nightmare that comes close to the reality that is war."

He put his arm around me, and we sat quietly by the fire watching the glow from the embers till they slowly faded away, and we retired for the night.

Mother woke midmorning to the sight of Jacob and me hovering over her bed. "Well, am I dead yet?" she asked.

"How ya feeling? You had a rough day," said Jacob.

Attempting a smile, she held her hand out to me. Grasping my hand, she answered Jacob with, "Well… I could be a lot worse if it hadn't been for an old friend."

Having felt a little barred, he asked, "Why is an old friend the last to know you were in town?"

With great affection, she answered, "Dad always said 'Jacob's done enough,' but please tell me how it is in a matter of life and death you just mysteriously show up. Keeping us alive seems to be your cross to bear."

Under heavy guard, the Pearl Cypress Mill became a fortress as we waited for mother to heal.

Aunt Lottie abhorred violence and was relieved when Uncle Jacob left law enforcement in Apalachicola for dry goods in New Orleans. They kept the house on Columbus and Laurel that Grandpa Kohler gave them for their wedding. Like the rest of us, they loved Apalachicola and frequently returned for visits.

It was in the name of civic duty that Jacob became involved in New Orleans' politics and now chaired one of the committees overseeing law enforcement. After surviving a war and a career filled with violence, his methods of law enforcement might be viewed by some as skewed, so it came as no surprise to us when a newspaper reported that early one morning, the head of Louis *Malocchio* Mechetti was found impaled on a fence spire in front of the crime family's home. The sign on the post read, "Assassins be Warned."

Clinging to the old ways, the family Mechetti was one of the few still paying homage to the family Agnusdei for adjudication. It did not bode well that both Etta and Malocchio died by beheading. Reports of shootings and stabbings were common enough and faded quickly from the public eye, but beheading smacked of voodoo and the dark arts. Frowned upon by the criminal families, decapitation always brought unwanted publicity shining light on their covert undertakings. Influential but unspoken were those who believed dark forces now cursed the Agnusdei home and all who entered, and Malocchio had fallen victim to these dark forces.

It was like a homecoming when Aunt Lottie arrived—until she discovered Uncle Jacob was shot, again. And for a while, the fur was flying. I had no idea this was the fifth time Uncle Jacob had been shot.

Lottie and Mother shared a deep and abiding affection that I felt was sure to hasten her recovery.

***

Early the next morning, we were jolted from our beds by a long, shrill, screaming whistle that suddenly began changing tone in a rhythmic sequence. Thinking aloud, I exclaimed, "What in the world!"

Then, just a second later, I recognized and began reciting, "Oh, I wish I was in the land of cotton, cinnamon seed, and sandy bottom. Look away, look away, look away Dixie Land."

It was, "Dixie," in all its spender, as Uncle Hatch made his grand entrance aboard the steamer *Charity*. Leave it to Uncle Hatch to have a buddy, who knew a guy, who had a friend, who was looking to sell a steam calliope, cheap. How he talked Aunt Bethany into this steam whistling conspiracy, I will never know, but there she was on the keyboard, pounding out a very rousing version of, "Dixie."

When it came to Hatch Wefing, Mother was just as big a child as her Captain. Grinning from ear to ear, she stumbled out of bed, grabbed her robe, and headed for the dock with Lottie in pursuit.

Bethany continued to play, and Uncle Hatch began to sing as Mother approached. Looking at her bandaged hand, Hatch pointed, but Mother shrugged it off as if it were nothing and joined in song. Raised on, "Dixie," they both knew all the versions, and soon it became a contest to sing a verse the other didn't know. Back and forth it went until Mamma started singing, "Buckwheat cakes and good...." Hatch was at a loss, struggling to remember the words. Mamma holding her arm up in victory finished with the verse with, "Strong butter makes my mouf go flit-ter flut-ter, look away, look away, look away Dixie Land."

Mother was starting to tire, so Uncle Hatch helped her onto a bench. Bethany approached, shaking her finger at Uncle Hatch, "Wipe that smile off your face, mister; you're just lucky this worked out, or you'd never heard the end of it."

Pleased as a puppy with two tails, Uncle Hatch said, "Why is it ya just can't say, 'You were right honey?'"

"Never gonna happen," Aunt Bethany replied. It was good to hear Mamma laugh so hard...; this was just the medicine she needed.

Uncle Hatch, now completely full of himself, boldly stated, "I kinda heard you might be having some troubles here, and by the looks of Pearl's hand, I heard right. So it got me to thinkin', with Jacob slowin' down in his old age, I'd best to head on over and take charge of the situation before things get out of hand."

Incensed, Jacob huffing and puffing called out, "Wefing, if your brain was dynamite, ya wouldn't have enough to blow your nose."

I was laughing so hard my ribs started to hurt. Hatch and Jacob were like brothers. They both knew if times got tough, they could count on one another. With a sincere handshake and a manly half embrace, they patted one another on the shoulders and reluctantly made up.

In a low voice, I heard Hatch confide in Jacob, "You're gonna love what I got on board."

What we didn't know is ever since Jacob learned of the contract on our lives, he and Hatch had been in cahoots, hatching a plan to cut the Mechetti crime family down to size. The scuttlebutt running rampant through lower levels of society led you to believe Malocchio was ceremoniously killed by a cult holed up at the Pearl Cypress Mill, and that he was being cut up and sold to the highest bidder one body part at a time, his murderous spirit being sold to the highest bidder for use in spells and potions. The cult would soon depart aboard the steamer *Charity*. Over the next few days, a steady stream of men began trickling into camp. Daily reconnoiters confirmed Mechetti's henchmen were gathering in force just down the road.

Chapter VII
Epic

I'd describe the first night of February not so much hot as it was muggy. Sleep eluded me as I lay listening to the hall clock ticking away the wee hours of the morning. With no breeze, the air in the house turned stale. So saturated was the air, every breath seemed a chore. Finally conceding defeat, I grabbed my robe and quietly slipped down the stairs through the piazza and strolled down to the dock. A near full moon illuminated the lake and surrounding area in a beautiful bluish tinge. As I approached the *Charity*, a hint of a breeze caught my face, and for the first time all night, I felt I could breathe.

"Morning, Miss," a voice announced.

Startled, but not alarmed, I replied in a pleasant voice, "Morning."

"Hope I didn't scare you, Miss. The name's Ben Worth." Striking a match, he held it up to a familiar face I'd seen around the mill. "I work for your mother here at the mill, and tonight it's my job to sit here and keep an eye on things. Muggy ain't it, Miss; I'll just bet you're havin' trouble sleepin'."

"You sure hit the nail on the head, Mr. Ben Worth."

Pointing to the *Charity*, he said, "Well, I'll just tell ya what..., the higher you climb, the better the breeze." Sitting down on a barrel, he lit his pipe and continued his watch. I climbed the ramp onto the *Charity* and found my way up to the pilot's house. Mr. Worth was right. The breeze off the lake was rejuvenating, and I soon found my sleep on a small bench behind the pilot's house.

I was sound asleep the morning of February 2nd when Uncle Jacob, Uncle Hatch, and a crew of three headed out onto Lake Pontchartrain aboard the *Charity*. She was still building steam to get underway when two smaller, faster, wooden hull steamers hiding up tributaries converged to intercept. The men crowded aboard the smaller steamers made no effort to hide an armory of weapons and making every effort to display their deadly intent.

Hatch nor Jacob announced their intent or departure to anyone in the family. I became alerted to the situation as the first shots struck the pilot's house just above my head, and the *Charity* fell under siege. Uncle Hatch yelled out through his loud hailer, "You bastards quit shooting holes in my boat, or I'm gonna start shooting back." His inappropriate remarks resulted in an unparalleled hail of bullets striking the *Charity*.

Jacob grabbed the loud hailer, shook his head at Hatch, and announced, "Police, pull your vessels to the dock and surrender to authorities." The reaction to Uncle Hatch's announcement was bad enough, but after Uncle Jacob's announcement, it was like being in a hail storm. I made my way to the front of the pilot's house to shield myself from the assault.

Captain Wefing ordered the *Charity* to come about and face its assailants. Jacob confused, yelled out, "What are you doing? Stick to the plan."

"Forget the dynamite, and get to the tarp," Hatch commanded, pointing across the deck. Hatch and Jacob ran toward tarps on either side of the bow's upper deck. Standing without fear, the bullets harmlessly ricocheted off the tarps. Whatever it was brought a grin to Uncle Jacob's face.

With grappling hooks in hand, men on the enemy steamers stood ready to capture the *Charity* and board her. All seemed lost until Jacob and Hatch threw the tarps, revealing two heavily armored Gatling guns. Opening fire, the big guns sent four hundred .58 caliber rounds per minute raining down upon the pursuing vessels, literally cutting them to pieces. Men were jumping into the water to escape the hail of bullets. There was a tremendous blast as a boiler aboard one of the steamers exploded nearly ripping it in half. I felt an impact on my face like being hit by a wave without water. Engulfed in fire, the other steamer would soon burn to the waterline. *Charity*'s pilot began yelling as he once again brought her about; a near miss on the starboard soaked Jacob in a shower of water, alerting him to a new threat.

An old, armored, Confederate gunboat took aim and fired a second shell, taking out one of the lifeboats. The .58s had limited effect on the heavy armor, and the steamer continued its approach. Hatch yelled to Jacob, "The bow—head for the bow. I'll cover you."

"Why?" Jacob yelled back.

"You'll know when you get there," Hatch yelled, pointing to the bow. Jacob ran to the ladder and slid down, holding the rails.

"Bring us about. Bring us about," Hatch yelled to the pilot, and he once again opened fire with the Gatling gun, suppressing the small arms fire aboard the gunboat, allowing Jacob to reach the bow just as a second shell from the gunboat's cannon took out the top of the pilot's house.

Hatch screamed, "Pull the tarp!"

Jacob couldn't believe his eyes. Without hesitation, he quickly aimed and fired. There are no word to describe the carnage that followed. The gun looked like the ones they were just firing, but this one was much, much larger. The armor plating on the gunboat was being ripped apart. After a minute of continuous fire, Hatch joined Jacob at the big gun. Signaling him to hold fire, he continued talking, describing the weapon as he reloaded, "47mm Hotchkiss Revolving Cannon. First round was armor piercing, and these shells are explosive tipped and ain't no old armor plate a match against six-nine rounds per minute," he boasted. "Fire when ready!" Hatch called out.

Reloaded, Jacob once again and opened fire, but this time it was different. Whatever Hatch had loaded in the gun was explosive. Round after round hit the gunboat, exploding on impact. Having ripped a hole in the armor, he constricted his fire, hollowing the boat out. Heavy debris fell like rain from the sky into the waters around the boat. When the gun was finally empty, nothing living could have remained onboard. Listing badly, it soon capsized.

The water became a flurry of activity as men frantically swam for shore. For every man swimming, another floated quietly on the surface. Drawn by the scent of blood, no one, not Hatch, Jacob, or Mechetti's henchmen anticipated the gauntlet of gators approaching from out of the swamps. Those who made it to shore grudgingly surrendered into the hands of waiting police officers. Militia waited down the road for those who stayed ashore. Unseen were the unfortunate few safely tucked away beneath a log or ledges tenderizing in some gator's meat hold.

We were soon back at dock; the men were cheering and ladies scowling as Hatch and Jacob took their bows, but it all became deathly quiet when I stood up in front of the pilot's house. Debris was falling from my hair as I bent over to brush the dust off my nightgown. Briefly losing track of time, I started to yell out, "Hurrah." Then looking up, in that moment, I realized the most devastating weapon of the day was not aboard the *Charity*. It was the look in Mother's eyes when she realized I was not in my room. I could see it in their faces; if given a choice, Hatch and Jacob would have preferred looking down the barrel of the Hotchkiss Revolving Cannon than to fall under the gaze of Pearl.

It was deathly quiet around the supper table. I had the feeling all was lost for the uncles until a knock at the door broke the silence. Mother stood, and in a commanding voice said, "Sit. I'll get it." No one challenged. The clouds were about to lift for Hatch and Jacob when from the door, she emotionally cried out, "Mother, Father, what are you doing here? Is everything alright?"

Leaping from my chair, I shouted out, "Grandma, Grandpa!" Running in, I joined mother in their warm embrace. Even as I approached, I couldn't help but notice something very different in Grandpa; he was standing taller, and his eyes were clear and attentive.

"What are you doing here?" Mother asked.

Excited, Grandma Caroline said, "News so good we wanted to share it in person." In dramatic fashion, she announced, "Pearl, your father's back." Grandpa blushed as everyone started staring at him. He hated being the center of attention and always strived to remain unseen at gatherings, a hard row to hoe when you're six foot five.

"Come in and sit. Tell me your news," Mother said. Taking Grandpa Kohler by the hand, she led him to the table, rubbing his arm, "It's so good to see you, Father."

I followed in tow, holding on to Grandma's arm. I saw Hatch and Jacob breathe a sigh of relief having received a temporary reprieve from Mamma's gaze. Grandpa noticed it too, and as he passed, he said, "What in the world have you two done now?"

With a look of pure innocence, Uncle Hatch pointed a quick finger in my direction whispering, "It was Olivia's fault." Grandpa was noticeably amused when he saw me rolling my eyes and shaking my head. It had been a while since we all sat around the same table. I knew this was the makings of a joyous reunion.

Mother asked Grandpa, "What's happened, Dad?"

Before he could utter a word, Gran jumped in, "Your dad's new doctor in Tallahassee summed it up best, 'The difference between medicine and poison is in the dose,'" she reported.

Grandfather, knowing he was off the hook, picked up a chicken leg, and with a smile on his face, he whispered, "Anybody gonna eat this?"

"Nah, go ahead, Grandpa. You eat all you want," I told him. Looking at one another, I saw a kindness I thought I'd lost forever.

With tears in his eyes, he grabbed me up, and he held me tight telling me, "I love you so much. Have I ever told you how happy you make me?" Suddenly realizing the chatter had stopped, we looked over and everyone was gawking at us, tearing up, sharing in our joy. Embarrassed, Grandpa winked at me and started eating his chicken leg.

All fired up, Grandma Caroline continued, "Quackery is the word that comes to mind when I think of that charlatan with his phony diploma, prescribing medicine he didn't understand. It was only Dysury and would have passed with time. He made it sound much worse, suggesting it could be a cancer, then prescribing an expensive tonic of his own creation, touting that if taken long term it was Dad's only hope. Turns out, what he gave your dad was a mixture of chloral and laudanum, not even made for the Dysury. It wasn't till after Dad started taking the mixture that he started having signs of the dementia. It's all my fault for not suspecting the medicine. The new doctor in Tallahassee took one look and told us Dad didn't have dementia but just a case of delirium brought on by that damn tonic."

Shocked, I said, "Gran, you said a bad word; you never say bad words."

Red-faced and mad as a hornet, she yelled out, "Well, I do when it comes to that damn doctor and his damn medicine...." Clutching a hanky, wiping tears from her cheeks, she continued, "I really thought... I was losing him," and she broke down crying. Fighting back the tears, she explained, "He started getting better right away...," pausing to wipe her eyes, "...and now he's back to his old self."

Grandpa couldn't stand it anymore. Gathering or no gathering, he loved her so much. Getting up from his chair, he held her in a loving embrace. The Bible speaks of the union between a man and a woman, and we all knew Grandma and Grandpa are what God had in mind.

After supper, the ladies moved toward the drawing room. Mother, who was still unwilling to forgive and forget, threw an evil eye at her miscreants as they headed out the doors to the piazza. I stayed with Grandpa and was surprised when they allowed me to sit in on the

66

conversation. Grandpa spoke first, "Alright boys, what have you done?" he asked.

Piping up, Jacob scowling, replied, "That's my question exactly. Hatch, you told me you secured the dynamite and rifles I requested."

Interrupting, Hatch blurted out, "And you know I did."

"Yes, yes you did, but where in the world did you come up with not one but two Gatling guns and, of all things, a Hotchkiss Revolving Cannon?" Jacob puzzled.

"Came in handy, don't you think? Aren't you glad we had 'em? Didn't work out better than your plan of pitchin' dynamite? What I know for sure is it saved a lot of holes in my boat, especially when the old gunboat showed up. You didn't even suspect they had a gunboat, did ya?" Hatch condescendingly stated. "Be prepared; that's my motto. Jacob, you may not know this, but in a situation like that, it's better to be over prepared than under. How do you feel about it?"

Jacob totally exasperated by Hatch's patronizing tone sat there red-faced and once again slowly asked, "Where did you get the weapons?"

Hatch nervously but still sitting tall, said, "I borrowed them from the Navy yard."

"Borrowed, you borrowed them? You're telling me the Navy loaned them to you?" Jacob questioned.

"The Navy had them removed from a gunboat and stored while they re-decked. They were in storage. It's not as though they weren't using them. Why not borrow them for a good cause?" Hatch reasoned.

"Does the Navy know?" Jacob inquired.

"I was planning on returning them tonight...." Hatch started to say when Jacob interrupted.

"So I can assume the Navy doesn't know," Jacob scowled.

"Can you imagine the paperwork I saved them by just borrowing a few guns without formally asking," Hatch responded.

Fuming, Jacob, keeping his voice down, preceded to tell Uncle Hatch, "They're going to put us in front of a firing squad and then hang us. You know this, don't you? Firing squad then hanging us to make sure we're dead."

"Not if you help me sneak it back into the warehouse tonight shitbird," Hatch responded.

"Shitbird! You have the nerve to call me a shitbird? You have got to be joking." Jacob was about to lose it when Grandpa interrupted.

Respected by both, Grandfather put an end to the squabble by simply saying, "Saddle up boys; time to invade the Navy."

Chapter VIII
With Great Respect

Excited I asked, "Can I go?"

Having just noticed me in the room, a look of terror came over Hatch and Jacob. Once again, they'd lost track of my whereabouts and now feared the wrath of Pearl.

Grandpa Kohler smiling looked down at me, "So much like your mamma it's scary. No, you can't go sweetheart, and for all our sakes, don't tell your mother."

"No need to worry uncles. I'll tell Mamma right after they shoot you but just before they hang you. But understand this, you better bring my grandpa home safe or Mamma will be the least of your troubles when I get through with you." They both smiled and chuckled, making me feel like one of the fellas.

Gran and Mamma were in bed asleep when just after midnight, way down by the mill, was heard the faint sound of the wagon pulling out. It was much louder from under the tarp where I was hiding. I couldn't believe they'd think, after hearing the plan, I'd let three, irresponsible, old men go on an adventure and not include me. It was a bumpy hour to the shipyard. We continued just past the shipyard to a warehouse in the commercial district of the docks. Hatch and Jacob opened large, double doors, and we pulled the wagon inside. Securing the door behind us, they lit several lanterns to work by.

"This isn't a Navy warehouse; what are we doing here?" Jacob questioned.

Hatch responded, "Jacob, I realize this is not the Navy warehouse, but we are close." Then in a patronizing tone, he pointed as if explaining to a child. "Did you notice this warehouse has a hoist? The hoist will make it easy to unload the heavy weapons onto those carts, so quit worrying."

Sarcastically, Jacob responded "And how does this in any way return them to the Navy's warehouse?

"It just so happens your old buddy Hatch just might know of a few loose boards that will let us into the Navy warehouse on the other side of that wall."

Dumbfounded, Jacob, once again struggled to unravel Hatch's slip shot reasoning. Red-faced, with a look of total exasperation, Jacob relented. "Oh, by all means, please continue. I am so sorry I asked, and I don't even want to know about you and your loose boards."

Using the argument as a diversion, I slipped out of the wagon and hid away until the need arose. If the need never arose, I'd simply hide back under the tarps and ride home. The weapons were very heavy, but thanks to the hoist, they were soon on carts lined up and ready to push into the Navy's warehouse. I heard Hatch telling them from here on out they needed to be very quiet so as not to alert the guards posted on the dock outside the Navy warehouse. Removing some boards, they slowly opened the door leading into the adjacent warehouse. Making as little noise as possible, they pushed the carts into the next building. I snuck up to watch through the open door but remained alert, ready to run back and hide under the tarps in the wagon. They were about to leave when suddenly a voice announced, "Advance," and the building lit up as a group of heavily armed soldiers hiding in the warehouse ran up and surrounded the carts.

Frozen like statues Grandpa and the uncles stood hoping against all odds not to be shot. Grandpa announced, "We are unarmed."

A voice from the darkness announced back, "Standing beside two Gatling guns and a revolving cannon. How 'bout you let me decide when you are unarmed?"

Jacob slowly stood and advanced to the front, holding his hand out from his sides to show he was unarmed. When all were searched, a man approached from the darkness. Jacob saluted, saying only, "Commodore." The Commodore ordered the men to stand down, and they moved away, standing at attention along the far wall.

"You men have been captured breaking into a naval facility, a very serious matter to say the least." Taking pause, one at a time, he looked into the eyes of the accused. "What I don't understand is which one of you figured, that after an epic sea battle on Lake Pontchartrain—using massive firepower—the Navy wouldn't suspect the weapons were taken from one of our facilities. This event was witnessed by police and militia and firsthand accounts from many who were arrested after they made their way to shore.

Commodores do read the papers you know…." Choosing his words carefully, "I could have you shot, but unfortunately, Commodores are not the only ones to read the papers. o do mayors, congressmen, and governors, and what you did taking down that crime family will buy them a lot of votes. You know they're all taking credit for what you did.

Now, knowing this, can you imagine what an embarrassment it would be for the Navy to admit incompetence in allowing their weapons to be stolen? The very same weapons used in your epic battle. Are we developing an understanding, solider?" He asked Jacob directly.

"Yes sir, word of this must never get out, sir," Jacob responded.

"Yes, gentlemen. I believe we have an understanding, but as you can see, nothing was stolen. The weapons in question are here in my warehouse. If the Navy ever found out these were the weapons, and I had captured and then let you go, I'd be up on charges and could lose my commission.

"So ask yourselves why I wouldn't just let you return the weapons and quietly slip into the night. My reasons are purely selfish. I didn't want to miss my only chance to meet the warrior," inches away from Jacob's face, he asked, "You are the warrior, aren't you?" Jacob stood silent. "The victors write the history, and the testimony of those trampled underfoot is lost to time." Staring into Jacob's eyes, he quietly stated, "April 6th and 7th 1862, I was a Confederate private at the battle of Shiloh. I'm willing to bet my career you were there too." Jacob remained silent and emotionless.

The Commodore continued, "I went down to the morgue to view the head of the assassin Malocchio. I understood there was a mark, and I had to see this mark with my own eyes. It is a mark like none other, a three-leaf clover like a club on a playing card. I've only ever seen it once before on April 7th, 1862.

"You know, the name, 'King of Clubs' will be lost to time because we were not the victors, but like me, there are those," pointing around the room, "who still remember the warrior who gave us hope. We fought for what we believed to be a noble cause, but as is the nature of war, a noble cause eventually becomes tarnished by truth and tainted by the greed of powerful men."

Placing his hand on Jacob's shoulder, "I am so very proud to meet the 'King of Clubs'. Take your men, and go in peace soldier, and don't worry; we'll lock-up." As he turned and moved away, he added, "Don't forget to take your young accomplice. It was because of the beautiful young lady you were never in real danger of being shot."

All three turned at the same time as I came out of the darkness and stood in the light, with my most timid of smiles. "Hi, y'all, I love you."

Having an immediate grasp of the situation, Grandpa Kohler was the first to speak up, "If Pearl looks in on her before we get home and finds her gone, our lives ain't gonna be worth living boys." Pointing to me he hollered out. "Climb in that wagon, girl; we got to get you home and fast."

We pulled into the mill a little after four o'clock and slipped quietly into the house. It was a relief to see the lights were out, a good indication that Mamma hadn't look in on me during the night.

***

It was near eight o'clock before the women could prompt the men to the breakfast table. Mamma got me up at six to help with breakfast, and I was one big yawn trying to keep my eyes open.

"What's the matter, Olivia? Didn't you sleep last night?" Mamma asked.

"Little trouble, but don't worry about me. I'll be fine," and she gave me a hug. Riddled with guilt, I knew Hell now lay in my path. I began wondering if confession really is good for the soul. Just then, the men joined us, relieving some of my tension.

Piping up, Grandma Kohler announced, "You boys workin' on banker's hours. It's getting kinda late for breakfast, don't you think?"

Grandpa grabbed her by the waist and pulled her down on his knee. "Woman, how 'bout you puttin' a little sugar on my lips to sweeten my coffee?" He gave her a little peck on the cheek. "Oh my, you are just too sweet; that's way too much sugar for one cup of coffee. Maybe I'll just have you stir it with your little finger."

Embarrassed, she scolded, "Michael Brandon Kohler, there are children present."

"I don't mind, Gran. It's no news to anyone you two are lovebirds," I replied.

"Such talk at the table. Mr. Kohler, you are incorrigible," and she gave him a little slap on the shoulder.

We were close to finally eating when Mamma announced, "I've decided to forgive you two miscreants," pointing her finger at the uncles, "unless you've done something imprudent since supper last night.... Well?"

"Well, what?" Hatch asked.

"Have you done anything imprudent since supper last night?" She asked again.

Blowing it off, Hatch scoffed, "Now, Pearl, what kinda trouble could we have gotten into overnight?"

Pointing at each, she threatened, "Knowing you, Hatch Wefing, and you, Jacob Foley, it is a real possibility, and don't you think for a second you're not included in this old man," pointing over to Grandpa. "I know exactly the trouble you're capable of causing. Mamma, now that he's got his wits back, you need to hold those reins tight." Then after a moment..., with affection in her voice, she added, "As irritating as you men are..., I'd like to keep you around a while longer." When no one was looking, Grandpa gave me a wink, and all had a nice breakfast.

Mamma and I sat and spoke most of the morning. I'd seen a lot of killing the day before, and she was fearful I might be scared. But she raised me well. Over the years, her lessons of good and evil and of life and death allowed me to justify the event and deal with the carnage. The concerns I voiced were more for Uncle Jacob. I could only imagine the Terrible War and darkness dwelling in his mind. I was thankful for Aunt Lottie and the solace he found in her embrace. Mamma teared up. She and Lottie were very close, and other than Grandpa, no one knew Jacob Foley better than Mamma.

Chapter IX
Smug Little Bitch

By the second week of February, Mother felt restored and was ready to meet with Carina. Contact was made, and Cyrus set the date with a time of one o'clock pm. It was overcast when we arrived, but even with clouds building off to the southwest, there should still be time enough for a meeting before the rain. Like thieves, we slipped in, stowing away between the offset of the back, garden fence. Hidden from the street and unseen from the house, we were exposed only to the vacant building at the far end of the alley. Just inside the garden, a trellis hid us from the view of those neighbors who might look down from their back windows.

I found a small knothole where unseen, I could get a glimpse of the backdoor. It wasn't long before Cyrus appeared. Laying an old quilt on the ground near the roses, he then carefully arranged the garden tools along the stone ledge at the front of the bed. As he worked, he asked, "Are you there?"

"Yes," Mother replied.

"Be forewarned. Miss Carina's mind is veiled today, and I'm afraid, at times, may seem of little use," he quietly stated.

"Veiled?" Mother inquired.

"Miss Carina is a seer, and even though you may question my words, be aware. I have raised her from a girl and stand convinced of her abilities. In one moment lucid and childlike, in the next, I implore your understanding," Cyrus pleaded.

Mother assured him, "We mean her no harm and will honor your wishes."

Cyrus, finishing his preparation, returned to the house. Holding the door open, he assisted Miss Carina down the steps and into the garden. Kneeling in front of the roses, she retrieved a set of shears and began pruning. "I'm so pleased you're here. It is rare indeed that I entertain company. Pearl, I know we've only met once, and while I may have appeared a smug little bitch, we were just children, and Aida was always watching. I sometimes dream the circumstance was different, and instead of fighting, we played wonderful games together."

It was the words, "Smug little bitch;" the very words in Mother's journal that were enough to give us pause.

"We haven't much time, and the story I tell is the unembellished truth of my nightmares. She pulled an old cutlass from the wall and hacked and hacked until her head hung on by one bloody thread. Men came and rolled her body into the carpet where she laid, threw her in the back of their wagon, and headed for the bridge. Holding the carpet tightly, they let go, and her body rolled out, but they didn't see the boat until it was too late. She became tangled in the rigging hanging above the deck, excepting her head; it popped off and bounced into the river. It was near a week before some boys fishing came across it bobbing next to a piling. They'd never have found it if her hair had not become snagged on a nail. If Mamma ever felt regret, I've never seen it."

Confused, mother interrupted asking, "You mean Aida...; don't you mean, 'If Aida felt regret'?"

"No... it was Mamma. Etta killed Aida. Aida thought she'd found the key and planned on keepin' it for herself. Mamma was furious 'cause she'd been looking for so long; she claimed to me it was an accident on account of, *you know my temper*, as if temper was ever an excuse for murder. It didn't help when the families started asking for Aida, feeling she was better qualified to pass judgments on their disputes. Her being dead would not bode well with the families. But did I tell you, Aida got it wrong, and now it's just me and Olivia who know the secret of the key.

And now we find ourselves in a tangled quandary with me knowing the what is the key but not the where is the key, and Olivia knowing where to find the what is the key, but not realizing she's already familiar with the key. It's just like in, *A Tale of Flodden Field*, 'Oh, what a tangled web we weave… when first we practice to deceive.'"

Carina was talking out of her head, making little sense to anyone but herself. It was all I could do to try and remember all the details of the conversation in hopes of sifting through them later. At times she seemed to be talking to us, but most time, she was waving her hands talking to the sky. Out of desperation, I asked.

"But I don't know for sure. Can you tell me again about the key?" I pleaded.

"No, no, no, you have everything you need and lots more than I had to begin my search." Sitting quite lost in thought, she softly spoke, "Airiana, so young and beautiful and full of love. I was gazing into her eyes when I first saw it; you know their eyes don't really follow you. They're just paint. How it happened, I don't know. The keys was in the first but not in the second." Quickly changing, she strongly urged, "Promise me you'll keep it from your Aunt Etta. That would be very bad, very bad indeed. Perhaps someday you might even consider coming back for me?

"After killin' Aida, Etta started worryin' about saving her own skin, not only with the police but with the families. She sent me to the police to spin a yarn, told me to identify the body as hers instead of Aida's and tell the police about how, 'she was always threating to kill herself,' to help reinforce an illusion of suicide. The police, they just took my word for it and marked it down as a suicide, reporting the head was severed by the cables in the rigging. When the head showed up a week later, it was in such bad shape, they just threw it in with the body and buried poor Aida in the ground, all the time believin' it was Etta. Poor Aida, she's dead. Better off for me; she was evil as they come but not nearly so wicked as Etta. She's been hidin' out here ever since, spending her time searchin' for the key. It unlocks a fortune you know, and with the key, she doesn't need me or anyone anymore. She keeps me around, holding onto the hope of me seein' the key, and I have, but I ain't so loony to be tellin' her."

Picking up the trimmings, Carina walked past us through the offset and threw the cutting into the alley. Before returning to the garden, she took our hands, and with tears in her eyes, thanked us for our visit. Once back in the garden, she suddenly sang out, "Oh, my captain, good strong butter makes my mouf go flit-ter flut-ter. Land of cotton, Cinnamon seed, and sandy bottom. Look away, look away, look away Dixie Land." Then turning back to the fence, she whispered, "I see your power child; seek your power. I am but a grain of sand at your feet." Turning, she made her way back and disappeared into the house. Mother and I sat dazed by the words of her song. The hair was standing on the back of my neck. What were the odds it could have been random?

A clap of thunder hastened our pace back to the carriage. A heavy curtain of rain followed close behind. We made it into the carriage just ahead of the deluge. Safely underway, we removed our sodden layers, but we both knew any chill we felt was nothing to do with the damp. Unspoken, with Carina's words seared in our minds, we looked to one another, pondering if not in a vision, how else she could have known? Mother, well known for her recollection, quickly retrieved a pencil and paper from her bag and began recording every word of our conversation so we could better review it later.

In response to her question, "I suppose you're right, Mamma," I answered.

"Right about what?" she questioned.

"About how the police will never believe two women from Apalachicola accused Etta of killing Aida and taking her place. I agree with you. To end this, we've got to find the key."

Confused, mother quit writing, staring at me in disbelief. "Olivia, that thought occurred to me, but I didn't say it out loud."

"Sure you did, Mamma. I heard you, plain as day," I told her.

In a very serious and sincere tone, she reiterated, "Olivia…, I'm telling you…, I didn't say it out loud."

I was looking to defend myself when I suddenly realized, I didn't actually see her speak the words. There was confusion in her eyes as she searched for a rational explanation. Finally relenting, she shrugged her shoulders stating, "Our imaginations are getting the better of us. We need to get back to the mill, sit down, and see if we can figure this out. Just one more stop before we head home. I need to run by the Charles."

Mamma was a woman of her word and hadn't forgotten she promised the steward two more gold coins for delivering those envelopes.

Pulling up in front of the St. Charles Hotel, she spotted the young steward and motioned for him to approach. "Yes ma'am, how can I help you today?"

St. Charles Hotel

"Do you remember me?" she asked.

"Yes ma'am, I made some deliveries, but I must tell you there was quite a stir just after you left the hotel. Three hard lookin' men snatched the guest register, went up, and ransacked your room.

I'd already moved your luggage down to the lobby for transfer to that new address you gave me, but I got to thinking…, those men might come down looking for your bags. I real quick took the tag off your luggage cart and switched it with another cart. I was right too; those three they came down and commenced to ripping those bags apart. No need to worry though. The police showed up just as Senator Randall L. Gibson was coming down the stairs, and I'll tell you what…, he wasn't any too happy seeing his wife's pantaloons and corsets strewn across the lobby floor. Needless to say, I don't think you'll be runnin' into any of those three for quite a while," he smiled.

I was only half listening, still reading Mamma's notes, but when I heard her chuckle, I looked up and smiled at the steward.

Mother thanked him, and because of his presence of mind, she placed four, twenty-dollar, gold, double eagles in his palm.

"Thank you, ma'am. I'm pleased everything was to your satisfaction. Please accept my card if you or your daughter should need any further assistance." Taking his card, she nodded to the young man as the carriage pulled away.

"Well the nerve of that young man," mother said.

Looking up from my reading, I puzzled, "I didn't hear him say anything out of turn. Was it something he did?" I asked.

"Well, the whole time he was speaking to me, he was looking at you," she stated.

Oblivious, I asked, "Why?" Worried I may have something green growing out of the top of my head.

"I'd say it was a nice-looking young man's way of getting a good look at an attractive young lady," she replied, with a smirk on her face.

"What?" I exclaimed in a skeptical voice, quickly looking back out of the rear carriage window. The young man was still there, watching the carriage pull away. With a smile on his face, he gave me a little wave. Seeming to have lost control of myself, I smiled and waved back. Turning back around, I sat with what must have been a stunned look on my face.

"I've always told you, you're very pretty. Didn't you believe me? Then with a smile on her face, she added, "We will be discussing this topic at length, young lady."

I assured her, "It's all in your imagination; it can't be."

"The color of your face indicates your body is in opposition to your mind," and hearing her say it just made it worse. I think it may have been her intention. I could feel myself blushing and getting all flustered or what Grandpa Kohler in German use to call being *verklempt*.

Mamma, in a more serious voice, tried to address the issue. "Olivia, it is a fact of life men think they're in charge, but love is a blinding force, and the facts will bear out, the young man standing back there in the rain, who doesn't even know your name, would more than likely jump off a cliff for you."

"No. What? Are you serious?" I asked.

"You must learn the powers of love works both ways. Just make sure, in the end, you have the upper hand. Granted…, you are a young woman now…, quite young, so you must learn to exercise restraint. But be forewarned, in the future, when he suddenly appears on the street with a smile and a warm greeting, it is not happenstance that brings you together," she warned.

"Oh, Mamma," I said, shaking my head in disbelief.

The carriage moved but a short distance when it suddenly occurred to me what she said was true. Even confronted with the fantastic mystery of the key, my mind kept going back to that young man's smile. It took some effort to get him out of my head and refocus on the key, but soon enough, a theory began to evolve.

***

Safely back at the mill, we sat around the supper table discussing our adventure with the rest of the family when Uncle Hatch bluntly stated, "She's nuts. You can't trust anything she says."

In Carina's defense, Mother fired back, "There's more to her than you give her credit for."

"What do you think, Olivia? She's two bricks short of a full load, isn't she?" Uncle Hatch prompted, trying to get me to back his position.

"What I think is we need to find the second painting," I told them. With everyone looking confused, I explained, "The second painting of Grandma Airiana holds the secret to the key. You remember, Mamma, Carina said, 'So young and beautiful and full of love. I was gazing into her eyes when I first saw it. You know their eyes don't really follow you, there're just paint. How it happened, I don't know. The key's in the first but not in the second.' There has to be a second painting, and we need to

81

find it. Mamma, you forgot to write down the part about the eyes being paint. The difference between the two paintings reveals the key." The argument went on, but mother sat quietly looking at me. I could tell by her gaze she was proud of my insights; she knew I was right.

Later that night, out on the piazza, Mamma announced a plan to search for the second painting. The first and most obvious place to begin was to send word to Cyrus asking if he knew of its whereabouts or if he could coax Carina into divulging its location, and when found, how we might get another look at the original in the foyer of the Agnusdei home. Word was sent early next morning, and it would be the longest week of my life waiting for a reply. Its arrival was a mixed blessing.

I started this. It was me who wanted to know my mother's family, but the look on mother's face as she read Carina's reply indicated her feeling were to the contrary. Carina wrote:

> "My Dearest Pearl,
>   Oliva's wish is to know her family, and for better or worse, I believe she has the right. Ask your question, seek your answers from the men appearing below, and be cautious.... Some of our uncles are indeed serpents."

Mother once wrote in her journal, "I did not comprehend the unseen powers that protected me. Their talk of the dead and spirits watching over me was quite unnerving. I preferred to think my protection came from the living, perhaps my mother's brothers, my four uncles, but what was the difference between the living and the dead? I knew less of my uncles than I did of the spirits."

Chapter X
Felix

In Italian it was pronounced Felice, in Sicilian Feh-LEE-cheh, here in America, it became Felix. The second oldest of my mother's uncles appeared first on the list. With so little known, Uncle Jacob checked police files searching for some insight. Regrettably, the files on Uncle Felix were extensive. The lowest form of criminal, Jacob dubbed him evil for hire. Our visit to Felix would leave a short but lasting impression. He lived in an old, dilapidated, shotgun house, one of many lining a street one block off the waterfront. Without a guide, we'd never have found it. Mother and I arrived in our carriage followed closely by a wagon filled with intimidating fellows who mother claimed were there to ensure a quiet, safe, and fruitful visit. Mother firmly instructed them to be alert but stay back, near the wagon, not wanting to intimidate Felix if he was willing to talk freely.

We just reached the door when a voice shouted out the window. "What the Hell you men doing out there? I got arms and won't think twice 'bout killing ya. What's this about? I ain't done nothin'."

Mother, backing up so she could be seen from the window, assured Felix, "Just here for a visit; wanted to ask you a couple of questions. Would that be all right?"

"You keep them, men, back, or there'll be big trouble. I guarantee it," Felix threatened.

"I promise the men will stay at the wagon while we speak," Mother assured him, gesturing to the men to stay in place. "You must be Felix. My name—'" is all she spoke before he screamed out.

"I recognize ya, you're an Agnusdei bitch if I ever saw one. You and your whelp. If you're here for Etta, go to Hell! I went to war for that witch and got nothin' but a knife in my back. She took everything from me, and I got nothin' left for you. Go away!"

Mamma said, "I'm here 'cause of Etta, not for her."

"Fine, you step inside, but keep them men back, especially them big niggers; got no use fer niggers."

Before we even broke the doorway, we could smell the filth that lay ahead. Outside, a variety of animal excrement lay thick on the porch under the windows. You could tell by the bones that he threw his table scraps from the broken windowpanes. Mother seemed to be in control, but I fought to keep from gagging. If soap and water ever touched this man's body, I would be surprised. The smell was overwhelming. My eyes began to water, and I held my hankie over my nose and mouth trying to avoid any contagion.

"Well… you're in. Ask y'ur damn questions so I might see the back of ya."

In retrieving my hankie, I lost track of Mother. She remained close, standing to my left, staring at the wall.

"Well, you gonna waste my time starin' at a wall?" he shouted.

I put my hand on Mother's shoulder, and she didn't break her focus. It was as if she had turned to stone. There were canes and a few old tools leaning against the wall and several old hats hanging from pegs just above, but it was one old, cracker hat holding her attention. The hat had seen its better days, and the wall peg protruded through a hole in the back. Mother slowly walked over and touched the feather in the band; then removing it from the peg, she smelled the inside.

"I ain't got time for this shit; get the hell out of my house," he shouted, and Felix grabbed my arm. I struggled against his advance, screaming at him to let me go when suddenly out of nowhere, Mother hit him squarely in the face with a steel coal shovel, knocking him to the floor. But it wasn't over. She kept striking him. Mother's eyes were wild as if her only purpose in life became beating this man. She held nothing back—these were killing blows raining down on him as fast as a rattler's strike. The men, hearing the commotion, crashed through the door but confused, found they were not needed.

I screamed at them, "Stop her! Please stop her. She's going to kill him." It took two men to hold her until she came to her senses.

The men held his arms to the floor, and Mother, with a coal shovel in one hand and the hat in the other, straddled his chest, waiting for him to come to.

"Crazy bitch!" were the first words to spew from his mouth. His nose broken and bleeding was a fine target for a tap with the coal shovel. As he was already sensitive, there was no need to hit him hard to make a point.

"Get these niggers off of me," warranted a second painful tap.

"This your hat? Where'd you get this hat?" Mamma commanded.

"Go to Hell," was not an answer and earned him a third tap. I think at this point, he began to understand the significance of the shovel. She began raising the shovel for another tap when he hollered out, "He was a friend of mine. It belonged to a friend."

"What was his name?" Thrusting the shovel, she feigned a strike.

"Aldridge, his name was Aldridge," Felix shrieked out.

"How did you know this man?" she demanded.

"We used to run cattle in Florida territory." Mother sat quietly for a moment, collecting her thoughts.

"So you don't like niggers?" she asked.

"Woman, last time I let a nigger touch me, I poleaxed him and left him for dead," he said scowling, spitting at the men holding him down.

Mother spoke up calling out her own name, "Pearl."

"Pearl. Pearl what?" he questioned.

"My name. My name is Pearl; do you know it?" she asked.

"Aw shit," in desperation, he struggled to escape.

"So you do remember me?"

"It wasn't me raped you, woman. I was waitin' at the boat."

"No… no…. It was Aldridge raped me. It was you, my uncle, my mamma's brother, let it happen. It was also you who poleaxed a nigger thereby killin' the man who raised me."

Sticking her finger through the hole in the back of the hat, she held it in front of his face. "This hole, in the back of your friend's hat, is where my mother put a bullet through his brain."

"Yeah, I knowed…. I seen it…. I was there…. Lucky shot is all," he said.

"Yeah, it was a lucky shot, and you ain't got to worry 'bout her 'cause she ain't here, but you do have to worry 'bout me," Mamma threatened.

Still rebellious, Felix challenged, "What I got to be scared of some privileged, little, rich girl from Apalach?"

"What you need to know Uncle Felix—it was me on the Albany. I slit your friend's throats and put a bullet in my own father's head, and was me that set her ablaze, and I'll just bet you were one of them Rebel Guard I saw running from the slaughterhouse toward the flames."

"Well, but don't' that make us even? I kilt your nigger, and your mamma kilt my friend," he reasoned.

"Yeah, in your head we must be even, but you square with this nigger holdin' you down?" she asked.

Defiant, he scowled, "I don't owe no nigger nothin'."

Mamma, holdin' the shovel just above his face, proceeded to tell him, "Fact is, I'm tired of hearin' the word nigger out of your mouth, so from now on, every time you say it, I'm gonna bash you with this shovel—one time more for every time you say it, and you up to four in a row now. So it might be best you use their Christian names. The man you poleaxed that night, his name was Ponder, and the man holdin' down yer left arm, his name is Mr. Jim. Mr. Jim here, he be Ponder's oldest boy. Now knowing this, you tellin' me you don't owe no nigger nothin. You killed this man's father. Now you need to thank these two men holding on to Jim 'cause right now, they the only thing keepin' you alive." Mother stood, throwing the shovel to the floor.

"Wait, wait! Don't you want me to answer them questions? Maybe we could make a deal?" he said in a panic.

"What spews from your mouth is a vile and wicked bile. Your words are pure poison. You have nothing to offer but your confession. As you once turned your back on me, I now turn mine on you and leave you to your fate." Mamma stood, took my arm, and we left.

The carriage ride was quiet. Mother, wringing her hands, wanted to speak but came up short of words. I had never seen pure blinding rage before today, never thought it possible in my mother. If the men had not held her back, Felix would already be dead.

Breaking the silence, I asked, "Was it the hat brought on your rage?"

As though in a trance, she answered, "I thought Aldridge was in my past. I thought I was in control. But all it took was a hat hanging on a peg. I couldn't look away. I knew the hat and its foul owner all too well, and everything he had done to me came flooding back.... The owl feather was the way the Rebel Guards were known to one another. Even after all these years, the stench of the owner still lingered. The smell was the final straw to break my back." Continuing to staring straight ahead, she began to recall events.

***

"A camp wagon had been sitting there for a week with a busted axel, but tonight, there was something new. As I approached the edge of the fire, I began to make out the pattern on Miss Charity's dress. She was crouched on her knees, her hands were bound with leather straps to the back wheel, and her head was covered with a canvas sack.

"I started to run to her when I was tackled from behind and forced to the ground. Suddenly, I recognized the smell. It was Aldridge. "'Member me girly? I come to make you a woman. This be a lucky night fer ya."

"I couldn't even scream; his weight crushed the air from my lungs. He gagged me with a rag and continued to rip at my clothes. When my back was bare, I could feel him probing with his hand and cock, trying to gain entry.

"I had never been so helpless and screamed, *Please God!* over and over again in my mind."

***

Falling silent she sat with a glazed look in her eyes. I knew this was the first time she had spoken of these events. I was honored that she felt she could share them with me. I felt that after all these years it was good for her to air out the past. I encouraged her to continue by commenting, "That wasn't the worst of it, wasn't it, Mamma?"

"No, my poor Ponder. Aldridge had struck him in the head with a shovel, knocking him unconscious. It was Elias who stopped the assault. He placed me in Charity's embrace, and cradling Ponder in his arms, he carried him into the shack and lay him on my cot.

The camp doctor walked out of the shack and spoke with Miss Charity. I quickly headed in and held Ponder's hand. The doctor did a fine job tending to the wound on his head where Aldridge struck him with that shovel.

Next morning, the best we could figure, Aldridge must have had a boat anchored up and escaped down the Brothers River. Otherwise, with the way he smelled, he couldn't have gotten away from the hounds.

Ponder remained unconscious for three days. Miss Charity and I took turns, never once leaving him unattended. We fed him broth so he might keep up his strength. On the third day, he awoke and seemed fine, but he wasn't fine, and over the next two weeks, his condition deteriorated.

Ponder began to lose control of his right side. It was as though he was split in half, one half no longer obeying his commands. Miss Charity had seen this before and called it by the name, "Severe Brain Attack." Much to my dismay, Ponder faded into a dream and passed away the last Sunday of October 1861.

Miss Charity and I picked a nice spot down by the Brothers River, under a live oak, to lay Ponder to rest. Miss Charity wept; she had become very fond of Ponder. I knew she was holding back her pain, trying to be strong on account of me.

88

September and October of 1861 marked one of the saddest chapters of my life. I don't think I will ever really recover from the events that transpired. To this day, my dreams are haunted by the pain and loss I experienced at the hands of one evil man.

I believe Felix is a coward and lied about waiting at the boat. I think he was there, cowering in the shadows, watching the perversion unfold. After the beating Elias gave Aldridge, there's no way he could have made it back to the Brothers River without help."

Suddenly coming back to her senses, she held my hands and asked for forgiveness. "I'm so sorry sweetheart, I know I must be frightening you. Please forgive me," she begged.

"There is nothing to forgive. Uncle Felix and his friend Aldridge were fetid to the core. I will lose no sleep over his fate. I know there is no justice, no court that would hold a white man accountable for killing a slave. Ponder deserves justice, and to my mind, Uncle Felix, knowing and not acting on your behalf makes him complicit and just as guilty as Aldridge for what happened to you. I like to think there's a special place in Hell reserved for men who rape children and those who let it happen."

Deep in thought, Mamma confessed, "How have I become so callous, so violent to think I can justify my role in murder and yet feel no remorse? What right do I have to judge? I wanted better for—"

Stopping her in mid-sentence, I announced, "No one, no one can possibly accuse you of being callous. You have devoted your entire life to the service of others. You are the most generous and devoted and loving teacher I could ever possibly hope to have. You have faced overwhelming odds and unthinkable circumstances your entire life, and I am so happy you are my mother. You have no right to call yourself callous in front of me because I will defend you against yourself, and I will win." Embracing, we both shared a well-deserved cry.

Chapter XI
Resurrection

We made our way back to the Pearl Cypress Mill where family distractions helped to ease the burden of the day's events. After a bath and a meal, we sat on the piazza watching a mist roll in over the lake. The quiet was to be short-lived when Grandma Caroline handed mother a letter. In the dim light, Mother struggled to read, but after a few lines, she leaped to her feet and ran into the light of the house. Grandma and I followed. Mother, ignoring our queries, studied the letter carefully; then holding the letter to her heart, she announced, "Olivia, pack a bag. We're leaving tonight."

Grandma responded, "Daughter, surely nothing could be so important. Can't it wait till morning?" Mamma lay the letter on the table, so Grandma and I could make sense of all the fuss, and she quickly headed to her room and began packing. The letter was from an old friend of my mothers, James Hancock. I remembered the mention of his name in both journals. He was the foreman at the turpentine camp where Mamma was reunited with Ponder. He was a just man who supported Mamma, Charity, and Ponder during their time at the camp. I thought back to Mamma's journal entry and the incident that must have spurred his letter. Mamma had written in her journal:

> *"Back at the wagon, I climbed on top of the barrels*
> *for a better view of the street. Impatient, I pulled a piece*
> *of chalk rock out of my bag and began drawing on the*

barrel tops. *I drew a picture of Hickory on the top of each barrel, and underneath the picture, I wrote the words, "Gator Rosin." I chuckled to imagine people trying to figure out what could be in a barrel marked Gator Rosin."*

I know it must have broken Mamma's heart to have left Bainbridge without saying goodbye to her new friend Odila. It was later in her journal that she recorded her conversation with James Hancock.

"During our conversation, I couldn't help but notice a most curious paper on his desk. I wouldn't have noticed it at all, buried among the scattered papers, but on this particular paper was a drawing, my drawing. I asked if I might see the paper, and he was very obliging, handing me one of the four copies he planned to post around camp.

The notice came from the Marshal's Office in Columbus, Georgia. On the notice was a rendering of my drawing of Old Hickory and below it the words, Gator Rosin. Mr. Hancock became concerned as I agonized over the document."

"What is it Pearl?" he asked.

"I know these children..." and I began weeping uncontrollably."

Mr. Hancock quickly sent a man to bring Miss Charity. Unable to speak, I laid the poster on his desk and wrote the names Odila and Zelig Freud, Bainbridge, Mr. Fredric Freud, Freud Mill Work Supply.

At a boat works in Columbus, the bodies of two children were found in the bottom of a rosin barrel encased in amber. The barrel was marked with my drawing and the words, Gator Rosin.

By the time Miss Charity arrived, I was no longer crying. I was angry. Darkness took over my mind, and I was absolute in my resolve. It was now between me and the Rebel Guard. I knew the best way to kill a snake was to cut off its head. My father, Dray, had to die. I was reminded of a passage, and I whispered it aloud:

"And I looked, and behold a pale horse: and his name that sat on him was Death, and Hell followed with him. And power was given unto them over the fourth part of the earth, to kill with sword, and with hunger, and with death, and with the beasts of the earth." Revelation 6:8

Although small, I was determined to bring the fires of Hell down on the heads of those responsible for bringing great evil among us.

I knew it was a sin to seek vengeance, but God was working too slowly to suit me. I wanted retribution for the deaths of Bella, Basher, Ponder, Odila, Ida, Mr. Freud, and Zelig and was anxious to place these evil men in judgment before the throne of God. And if God were to judge me evil by thought or action, I was willing to accept my place in Hell beside my enemies. My only vindication might have to be that no one else would die by their hands.

The envelope from James Hancock contained a brief note and a newspaper clipping.

Pearl,
I remember all too well the day you saw the notice on my desk; your reaction to the death of the Freud family touched me deeply. When I saw this in the paper. I felt you should know.

With great affection,
James Hancock

The newspaper clipping reported the city of Bainbridge was saddened by the announcement of Mr. Freud, his wife Adeline, and their niece Odila, moving back to Columbus, Georgia. I questioned how this could possibly be true. Grandma Caroline, holding a hankie over her mouth, began to cry, and I followed her to mother's room.

"I'm coming with you," Grandma announced.

Mother was beside herself and joyful beyond words. She and Grandma hugged. I heard Grandma whisper, "I hope against all hope this is true. We'll discover it together, and if it is true, I am so happy for you."

I knew the death of Bella had devastated my mother but it was the death of Odila that drove her to murder. I believe their meeting at the spring was an ordinance of God. Akin from the moment they met, Mother would never allow herself to be bonded to any one friend so closely again.

Hardly able to contain herself, she continually called for a carriage as she packed her bag, occasionally hollering out for Grandma and me to hurry along. We knew by the determination in her voice, there was no postponing the inevitable. She would be leaving tonight, with or without us. We had a rather long wait at the rail station, but once aboard the train, the Pullman Sleeping Car provided more than an adequate accommodation.

***

Hidden by the darkness, a powerful steam locomotive pulled us along the rails, blowing its whistle at crossings and making stops for passengers and fuel. I tried to wake at every station, noting the names of cities and towns as a record of my passing. Unlike mother, I found trains to be a pleasant mode of transport, finding comfort in the rocking motion of the cars, the rhythmic clacking of the wheels, and the distant puffing of the engine. The food provided in the dining car was not unlike a fine restaurant. We changed trains just shy of Montgomery, transferring to a smaller line that ran into Columbus. But no matter to me, it was all an adventure. Near to four hundred miles traveling at thirty to fifty miles per hour, depending on the grade, and taking into consideration stops, the trip took about fifteen hours.

Mother made inquiries at the station in Columbus, and a carriage dropped us at a hotel not far from the Freud Mill Work Supply where we could freshen up before making introductions. At the hotel, Mother sat at the desk creating a calling card to announce our wish to visit. She folded the upper left-hand corner of the card to indicate we would arrive in person—unfolded indicated a servant would be sent. The reply came quickly and was an open invitation to arrive without haste.

Mr. Freud was a successful businessman, and their home was a reflection of his wealth. A maid opened the door to greet us but was moved to one side as Adeline Freud hurried out to greet us in person. Holding Mamma by the cheeks, she asked, "Could you possibly be the Pearl Ida had spoken so fondly of in her last letter?

"Yes, I am Pearl," Mamma replied. Hugging her tightly, Miss Adeline cried out, "I have been many years asking for a miracle, and now I truly believe the miracle has arrived. Please come; come inside for a most welcomed visit."

"Is Odila here? Can I see her?" Mamma asked, hollering out, "Odila!"

You could see in her eyes, Miss Adeline shared Mother's excitement, but holding Mamma back, she pleaded, "Pearl, you need to know a few things before your visit. Please, may we speak?" and she directed us into the parlor.

Mr. Freud left work to receive us and rose to his feet to greet Mother, gently kissing her hand. "Welcome, to our home, Miss Pearl, and who are the ladies in your company?" he inquired.

In her excitement, Mother forgot her manners; apologizing profusely, she made the introductions.

Miss Adeline motioned us to sit, inviting us to take tea. Mother began crying, telling Mr. Freud, "You are so much like your brother, and I can tell by the smells coming from your kitchen, you favor meat pies."

Miss Adeline weeping, holding Mamma's hand told her, "It's Ida's recipe."

Unable to speak, Miss Adeline turned to Mr. Freud motioning him to begin. "Over the years, Odila has become mute, understandable having watched her mother murdered. I am of course assuming you know of that terrible day in Bainbridge?" he asked.

Mother, in tears, nodded yes. "It was early that morning my brother and his son Zelig were abducted from our mill store. When they did not soon return, Ida sensed something was amiss, and when strange men approached the house, she hid Odila away in a small room beneath the stairs. It was Betsy Turner, God rest her soul, a local shopkeeper's daughter, making early deliveries that was mistaken for Odila—a fact not reported in local papers.

"Adeline and I were joyous to find Odila alive and embraced her into our family, but her scars went deep, for it was through the louvered door below the stairs, she'd heard her mother's cries for help as she was beaten and raped and then stood witness as her mother's throat was slit. We are so fortunate she listened to her mother and remained silent, but to Odila, remaining silent is her greatest regret. Not long after, she wished she'd cried out and died at her mother's side. Nothing we said will convince her otherwise." Stopping for a moment, he collected himself.

Then continuing, "It was five years after the war that the post office found a tattered and faded envelope addressed to our store in Bainbridge, and some kind soul forwarded the letter to our store here in Columbus. The return address was unreadable, but it was unmistakably to the attention of Miss Odila Freud. We shared your letter with Odila, and although she remained silent, it was the first time she smiled since the murders. But we knew of Pearl long before the letter arrived. Ida was very taken with Odila's friend and wrote to tell us about you.

"We don't know what Odila's reaction will be. Please understand; her memories are faded, and her pain is rooted deep.... She may not recognize you at all," he warned.

"I simply must see my friend; please take me to her," Mother pleaded. Adeline stood and led us upstairs. Adeline opened the door for Mamma but stayed with Grandma and me on the settee in the hall. From here we could listen without overwhelming Odila.

Odila, with a brush in hand, was sitting at her vanity, gazing into the mirror. She changed her focus, watching Mother approach from behind. Without saying a word, and just as Odila had done for her at the spring head years ago, Mother motioned, offering to brush her hair. Odila's hand turned out, and Mother took the brush and gently began stroking her hair. It was a reunion without words, and we all sat in, half hopeful of the outcome.

Near an hour passed before Mother leaned over and looking in the mirror asked Odila, "I know I am much older now, but do you still see your Liebling?" Suddenly, Odila became inconsolable, clutching at Mamma's sleeves, she pulled her to her knees. Throwing her arms around Mamma's neck, she continued to wail, sobbing bitterly. Adeline was beside herself, and with great joy, she announced, "She's finally grieving."

Mother never left her side, staying with her day and night. Mamma would sometimes invite me to sit with them while she told stories of her adventures, some of the adventures were ones she and Odila had shared.

My favorite was when mother recalled their first meeting at the spring head outside of Bainbridge Georgia. I loved that story.

Mamma started the story just like she had written in her journal, but this was much more entertaining than rote because Mamma was standing and acting out each part. She started by shouting out:

"Suddenly, a blood-curdling war whoop sent chills down my spine and woodland creatures scurrying for cover. Expecting an attack, I turned just in time to see a slip of a boy leap naked from the highest rock ledge and splash into the springs. I doubted he could have been much more than three or four, but he could swim like a fish. He finally came up for a breath, and I was ready to ask what he was doing here all by himself when a young girl about my age walked out of the wood and onto the rocks.

"Speaking in broken English, I could tell she was apologizing for her brother's behavior. Then, in a stern voice 'Zelig Freud, you must behave,' she shouted. Zelig disappeared back under the water, unwilling to listen, acting as though he hadn't heard her at all. I shook my head and smiled at her. I knew this was a woman's way of saying: I understand—men are all alike.

"She approached down the rock steps and signaling with her hand, made a gesture as though brushing her hair. I handed her my brush and comb, and she began to tame my tangles. 'Odila,' she spoke, smiling, pointing at herself with the comb.

"'Pearl,' I said, returning your smile."

Odila began tearing up as soon as she heard Zelig's name, I think Mamma was trying to get Odila to remember the good times and associate Zelig with a wonderful memory and not the tragedy to follow. It worked and when Mamma had finished, she spoke kindly of Zelig, and together they mourned his loss but at the same time celebrated the time they had spent together.

The mood was turning a little too somber when suddenly Mamma sprung up and asked Odila, "Do you remember the first time I met your father. I will never forget. It is etched in my mind.

"You had invited me to dinner, and I'll tell you what, there is no doubt in my mind that with the heavenly smell of your momma's meat pies drifting through the streets, I could have found your house from a mile away. The first thing she did was give me a hug and pinch my cheeks just like she had known me forever.

"Your papa was late. Miss Ida excused his absence by stating the fact that, 'only Mr. Sanborn at the Estahatchee Mill could have kept him away from his favorite meat pies.'

"I had only had a couple of spoons of beans for my breakfast and was starved, but after scarfing down a dinner of three of your Momma's meat pies, I felt like a tick ready to burst."

Odila chuckled as Mamma walked around the room, with her cheeks puffed out acting like a tick ready to burst. Continuing on with the tale, "Your Papa returned home midday, and you and Zelig ran to meet him. Your papa smiling from ear to ear, grabbed each of you, hoisting you into the air and giving each of you a hug and kiss before he put you down, all the time calling you and Zelig, 'my little *Lieblings*.' But then turning to me, he stood tall and asked, 'Momma, has the stork brought us another child while I was away'?"

"No, no, this is good friend. Her name is Pearl," Miss Ida replied.

"I saw the look in his eyes and started to flee, but he grabbed me and tossed me into the air shouting out, 'Three *Lieblings* is much better than just two'.

"Odila do you remember the look of sheer terror on my face when he hoisted me into the air?"

Odila did remember, and when Mamma tried to make the face again, Odila broke out laughing.

"Then he kissed me on the cheek and gave me a big hug. You and Zelig were laughing out loud at the stunned look on my face. But it wasn't over yet. He grabbed your Momma and began dancing around the room," and with that said, Mamma began twirling around the room as if dancing with a partner.

"Then your father commanded, 'Break out the cherry cordial for the children and the wine for us, Momma. We sold the new machines to Mr. Sanborn. We must celebrate,'" he shouted.

"Even full of meat pies, I was still able to find room for cookies and cherry cordial. I couldn't understand the conversation when it would drift into German, but I didn't have to speak the language to sense the excitement and join in the celebration.

"Before I left, I remember asking you, 'What's a *Liebling*?' and you told me, 'It is a darling or a sweetheart. It is you Pearl. You are my Liebling.' This moment was one of the happiest memories of my childhood, and I owe it all to you for inviting me into your family." Odila and Mamma embraced for the longest time while I sat and tried to control my tears.

After a week, Odila began speaking. Eventually recalling her ordeal, she allowed Mamma to share in the burden of her pain. It was good for Mother because, as she suspected, Odila recognized Dray's voice and confirmed his involvement. It was important to her that Odila knew this evil man was dead, and he had died by her hand. Mother was pleased Odila didn't feel any ill will toward her for bringing evil into her life. After the second week, she was able to sit on the porch where Mamma continued pushing tragic memories into the past.

A month later, they both went missing, returning late in the day arm in arm, laughing and carrying bags of art supplies, supplies mother felt she needed. Adeline and Mr. Freud were noticeably worried. Odila, seeing the concern on their faces embraced them, thanking them for their kindness and for taking on such a burden. There wasn't a dry eye on the porch when Odila came to this realization.

I think it was in that moment that Mother had an epiphany of her own and finally forgave herself for having a murderous father. But reality crept in, drawing her back to New Orleans, and she once again began addressing the threat and even voiced a concern for Carina's wellbeing. The next day she broke the news to Odila, announcing our departure but promising to return, so together they could travel down river to Bainbridge and draw on the stones at spring head where they first met, perhaps even share some beignets at the Frenchman's Café.

Although unspoken, we all knew it was to continue the healing and visit the graves of her family.

Chapter XII
Perilous Journey

Mother announced before heading back to New Orleans, we may as well stop a few days back in Apalach just to make sure everything was in order. I think her decision may have been influenced by Grandma Caroline's fretting about being away from home so long.

At noon next day, we boarded the Sternwheeler *Bertha Lee* for the trip down river. I was standing on the upper deck of the stern when the whistle blew and the great wheel began pushing a 120' steamer away from the dock, an impressive sight indeed, taking my breath away. I thought, *This is why my mother admired these old boats.*

Mamma insisted we all sit on the bench in front of the pilot's house and take in the majesty of her great river. "After all," she said, "I am the queen of these watery lands."

I turned to Grandma and assured her, "I figured with scheduled stops we should be back in Apalachicola in about fourteen hours." Grandma, of course, commented on how smart her granddaughter was.

We were having a grand old time. We ate our supper in the open air beneath a starry sky where even the *Bertha Lee*'s simple fair became a banquet. Tuning in at eleven, we were sound asleep in our cabin when just after midnight, a tremendous blast shook us from our beds. The boiler of *Bertha Lee* exploded, and a perilous journey began.

Bertha Lee

Abruptly, the *Bertha Lee* began to list, and we could feel the great steamer turning sideways in the current. Mamma shouted out, "Get dressed!" Seeing me reach for a bag, she called out, "Olivia, only the bare essentials, just the clothes on our backs we have to get out of here." Quickly dressing, we hurried out onto the walkway of the upper deck. The boiler explosion blew the hot coals from the fireboxes high into the air, and smaller fires appeared everywhere.

Turning in the current, the wind suddenly carried the smoke from the stern toward the bow, filling every compartment with hot, blinding fumes. Mother and Gran had seen this before and threw a wet towel over my head to help me breath. Instinctively, they linked hands, and with me in the middle, we moved away from the fire toward the lifeboats at the bow.

Gripping the rail, we scrambled down the stairs to the main deck. It was to our good fortune the *Bertha Lee* continued turning in the current; the wind shifting in our favor cleared the decks of blinding smoke. The light of the fire illuminated the river to the shore, casting an eerie flickering light upon the trees. Debris interlaced with the bodies of the dead floated alongside, adding to the panic.

Made of lighter pine and coated with rosin, the *Bertha Lee* was not long for this world. We needed to get off quickly. There was room for

102

mother and me in one boat and Grandma Caroline in another. We said a hasty goodbye and vowed to find one another on shore.

We were rowing away when just off the port bow, I spotted movement in the water. "Man overboard," I yelled, pointing in the general direction of the distress. It appeared out among the wreckage someone was struggling to stay afloat, fighting to get to the surface through the debris. Changing course, the oarsman moved toward the commotion. Holding on to the anchor rope with one hand, I leaned out over the side of the boat. Feeling beneath the water, I searched for the survivor. Finding what seemed to be skin, I tried to grab hold but could find no purchase. Instead, my touch seemed to direct the poor soul back toward the surface. Breaking the water, I was startled to find my hand atop a large, dark head, and from its mouth suddenly spouted a mist of water in my face. Then drawing a breath, it dropped back below the surface. Mamma yelled out, "Do you need help?"

Embarrassed, I shouted back, "Sea Cow…, it's just a Manatee," and the oarsman changed course to shore.

Mamma asked the oarsman, "Do you know where we are?"

"Moccasin Slough, Ma'am," he responded.

Mamma seemed relieved, but finding no comfort in the name Moccasin Slough, I asked her, "How is this good news?"

"Look ahead," she said. Turning to the bow, I was surprised but pleased to see lanterns on small boats approaching from shore.

"Who are they?" I asked.

Pointing in the direction of the incoming boats, she told me, "We're near Wewahitchka. They must have heard the explosion and seen the fire. The people of Wewa are coming to our rescue; it's to our good fortune it happened here."

The landing became visible as we approached the shore. A couple of flatbed wagons with men and emergency supplies arrived as we stepped off the boat.

One of the draymen, dropping a wooden step by the wagon, hollered out, "Board here ladies. The women in town are getting things ready to give you some comfort after yer ordeal. The men will row down river and try 'n' find yer possessions, at least them things that floats, and o'course, look fer yer dead—least maybe them who gets tangled up in the cypress knees. That way, we can give 'em a proper sendoff and burial."

His speech was crude, and I didn't find comfort in his words, but his heart was in the right place. I knew he meant well. Once loaded, it was a short ride to the church in town where the ladies rushed up and began hovering around catering to our every need. At the front of the church, for those who suffered loss or were missing people, the preacher was offering comfort in prayer.

Although we were not long parted, it was a joyous reunion when Grandma Caroline arrived on the next wagon.

Five lives were lost in the initial blast, three more died during the night as a result of their injuries, and most of the rest were minor burns and scrapes needing only time to heal. For the families of those who died, the scars inside were more permanent.

It had become safer over the years, but river travel was still a gamble. It was known the average life of steamers was three to five years before they would blow up, burn to the waterline, or hit a snag and sink. Every year the river claimed a few more lives. For men of commerce, it was a cost of doing business, and for the rest, the price of river life. I felt fortunate having had passage on many steamers that this was my first perilous journey.

The people of Wewahitchka opened their hearts to us, spending the rest of the night giving aid and comfort. The offer of payment would be an insult, diminishing their gift to nothing more than commerce. We never gave it a second thought; one expects nothing less of river folk.

By eleven o'clock next morning, the *Naiad* was at the landing waiting to carry us home. We stood on her upper deck watching as the last coffin was carried aboard. Mother was unusually quiet, and Gran was fretting, nervously wringing her hankie. In hopes of changing the mood, I announced, "Someday I'd like to come back and search for the city of Iola."

NAIAD

Mother who had been there as a girl recalled, "When I passed through just before the war, Iola was a vine-covered ghost town, but some of the tracks from the old St. Joseph & Iola railroad were still there. There are two Iola's you know; the first dates from 1836 and was pretty much abandoned by 1845. The Iola you see today started up later about two miles west of the original town, and for some time, they kept the rail between the two Iola's in repair. I understand today the new Iola is struggling to survive and may go the way of its namesake. Visiting the old ghost town sounds like fun. I'd be pleased to be your guide."

"I was hoping you'd offer. Do you remember much about the old Iola?" I asked, prompting her to give her recollections of the town.

"When I passed through as a girl, it was a ghost town, abandoned long before I was born. According to the stories, I've heard the old Iola started as a small, river town back in thirty-six, and by the end of thirty-eight, I understand there was a grist mill, a steam sawmill, hotel, and post office.

It was also along about this time that St. Joseph began searching for direct access to the Apalachicola River, and all their surveys pointed to Iola. A boom for both towns, they began laying the track for a new St. Joseph & Iola railroad. Upon completion, it would be the third steam railway to be built in the state. In anticipation of the coming prosperity, by thirty-nine, Iola had already added two warehouses and improved the wharf to accommodate all those steamboats and all that cotton soon to be passed through their city. Running the track to Iola would be St. Joseph's latest attempt to bankrupt Apalachicola by pilfering our cotton trade. But it was not the first time they'd tried.

When it came to commerce between Apalachicola and St. Joseph, there were times you could have cut the tension with a knife. The first steam rail in the state was the Lake Wimico & St. Joseph line. It was only about nine miles long. The plan was to divert the cotton packets from the Apalachicola down the Jackson River then through Lake Wimico to the railhead at Depot Creek. Problem was Lake Wimico was always more of a bayou than a lake, shallow at best. Silt often grounded steamers trying to reach the railhead, and this first attempt at stealing our cotton trade soon failed. St. Joseph's second attempt pushed a rail to the northeast to the Dead Lakes into the town of Iola, giving them direct access to the Apalachicola River. Iola soon became a railroad town whose sole purpose was to pull the cotton off the river, load its ill-gotten booty onto the St. Joseph & Iola rail, and send it to the docks of St. Joseph. But 1841 changed everything."

"That was the year of the Yellow Fever, wasn't it?" I asked.

With a proud look on her face, she announced, "So you do listen to your old mother sometimes."

"The outbreak in St. Joseph started in May of 1841. Within two months, they filled three cemeteries with Yellow Jack's victims, but digging one hole at a time wasn't fast enough, and with bodies piling up, they stopped digging graves and started digging trenches. It was for the best, no other choice. With contagion running rampant, they needed to get those bodies underground.

"After the fever of forty-one, there was a hurricane the same year that destroyed much of the waterfront. Not long after a fire broke out destroying even more of the city, then in forty-four a powerful hurricane called *The Great Tide* wiped St. Joseph from the face of the earth. Some in Apalach believe the Great Tide was the finger of God coming down to destroy the city of St. Joseph, the city Apalachicola had deemed, 'the sin city of Florida—the wickedest city in the United States.'

"Was it just coincidence Iola suffered a similar fate? The river was becoming shallower, and the channel was moving away from Iola. The fever of forty-one took its toll on the community. By forty-two most of the rail was sold for scrap. The Iola post office closed its doors in forty-five."

Grandma Caroline interrupting said, "Daughter, your story is all well and good, but you also have to remember your Daddy's family lived in St. Joseph and perished in the epidemic. Like many others who also lived there, they considered St. Joseph to be the 'Queen City of the South.' It was never just about stealing the cotton trade, was it?"

"You're right of course, but doesn't it make a more dramatic tale leaving that out?" Mamma laughed.

Grandma questioned, "You gonna tell Olivia what it is your Daddy thinks was the real reason St. Joseph and Iola failed, or you want me to?"

"Naw, I'll tell her, Mamma. It's not nearly so dramatic as most of my tales." Then looking straight at me with a slight grin, she said, "But I can still tell it better than your grandma can."

Piping up, Grandma said, "Aw pshaw, I can spin a tale better than you on my worst day."

Mamma continued, "Fact is there were many reasons why St. Joseph and Iola failed, and although the fever played a big role, there was an unseen monster lurking in the hearts of men, and its name was greed. Fortunes were spent, local people invested their life savings in those railroad enterprises. But in the background, the banks were printing far more money than they could back up in gold and silver, and in thirty-seven, there was a panic, and the banks began to fail. The state defaulted on the loans from the federal government, and the economy was thrown into turmoil. In the years to follow, local banks began calling in loans, but with no money to settle the debt, the land itself became forfeit and was sold away for as little as twelve cents on the dollar.

"The thing you have to understand about commerce is while many will lose everything, there will always be a greedy few who invest their time and money in failure, and like vultures, they sit poised, ready to reap a profit from the carcass of failed investors. They justify their fortunes behind the facade of *good business.*

"It's your Grandpa Kohler's opinion that even without the economic turmoil and the epidemic, the St. Joseph & Iola rail was doomed to fail. Their fees were high, nullifying the benefit of the railroad in the first place."

Finding her words disturbing, I told her, "I think that may be the scarier of the two stories."

Gran, shaking her head yes, responded, "If I might borrow from Robert Burns…. It is 'man's inhumanity to man,' I fear the most." We both stood with our mouths open, staring at Gran who just quoted Robert Burns.

"What are you staring at?" she asked. "I read all the time," she stated. Then acting all dramatic and haughty she finished, "It's just that I am too busy baking pies and cakes for my princess Olivia to do a lot of quoting." We all began laughing so hard I like to have split a side.

It was fifty-two miles from the landing at Wewa to the Apalachicola Bay, so God willing, we'd be home by three. I told Mother and Gran, "I never thought I'd say it, but I've been away too long, and I'm missing the old town."

Wrapping their arms around me, we sat and watched the miles drift by. When Apalach came into view, I again puzzled, "I still don't understand what has changed and why I am so anxious to be back in this old town."

That's when Grandmother Kohler once again said, "Absence makes the heart grow fonder," and for the first time, her saying made sense.

Chapter XIII
Father Giuseppe

We disembarked, and as we walked through town, everyone was waving and wishing us welcome back. Grandma was anxious to check in at her Florida Boarding House to make sure everything was business as usual, and she wanted to stop by the Trinity Church to say a prayer for those who lost their lives. As we walked away, Grandma hollered, "Olivia, if you bring me some rosemary from your garden and come over in about a half hour and help me pluck a hen, I'll roast it for our supper."

Mother smiled at me, and said, "Sounds like a good deal to me."

Hollering back, I said, "Sounds good to me, Gran," and with that settled, Mamma and I headed home. Our walk took us up Columbus Street to Grandma and Grandpa's house on the corner of Columbus and Cedar. Make a left on Cedar, and we were in the same block, just down the street on the corner of Market and Cedar.

As we approached the house, it became apparent we had company. Handing me her bag, she freed her right hand sliding it into the pocket of her skirt. She didn't think I knew, but I did; she was gripping the handle of her revolver. We both jumped when old Mrs. Goodlett burst on to her porch and headed down the walk to gossip.

"Well, I was a wonderin' when you'd decide to come home." Whispering under her breath, "You got a visitor. He's been poppin' in every so often over the past two weeks. He seems to like your porch. He's spent hours there just sittin' and waitin'. Anybody else, I'd called the law, but seein' he's a priest and all, I figured... what's the harm?

"Y'all are still Episcopalians…; ya haven't gone away and come back Catholic have ya?"

A little perturbed, Mother abruptly responded, "No Mrs. Goodlett, we're still Episcopalians. We really must go. We have a visitor waiting."

Mrs. Goodlett, feeling short-changed and still wanting to gossip, called out as we walked away, "Well, you be sure and stop back by soon, so we can catch up, and you can tell me all about your visitor."

"Yes, Mrs. Goodlett…. Very soon Mrs. Goodlett," Mamma said.

Rising to his feet, the man smiled a pleasant smile and greeted us as we approached, "Good afternoon ladies. Forgive me for postulating, but one of you young ladies has to be Miss Pearl?"

Mamma smiled back but was anything but sincere; she wasn't ready to drop her guard over the backhanded compliment of a stranger, not even one wearing a collar.

Confirming, "Yes, I am Pearl."

"Please forgive me for not first introducing myself. My name is Father Joseph. Back in New Orleans, many of my older parishioners call me Father Giuseppe. Pearl, I am your uncle. Mamma turned pale as she gazed at his collar but was still unwilling to remove her hand from her pocket. I shared her pallor, for I recognized his name from Carina's list, but I also remembered, beside his name, she had drawn a small cross.

Being very blunt, she asked, "What brings you here?"

"Let me assure you, my intentions are good and honorable as I am certain your neighbor Mrs. Goodlett and her extensive family can attest. I have been well behaved here on your porch, but I'm afraid my visit carries a sadness.

"I hate to be the bearer of bad news, but your Uncle Felix was found beaten and drown, floating in the waters near his home, and I understand you were one of the last people to see him alive. I'm just here to try and find out what might have happened. Please don't think for a moment I believe you had anything to do with the murderous event. I know my brother was not a kind man and had many enemies. I guess I'm just searching for my own peace of mind, hoping in the end, he may have shown some glimmer of redemption.

"Might you consider joining me on the porch for a visit? I know you must be tired after your journey. I can always return later if later would be better."

"Olivia, why don't you run down to Grandma's, and let her know we will be four for supper, and help her prepare two hens."

Appearing excited, Father Joseph responded, "Thank you so much. I know we both have lots of questions. Why don't I sit here on the porch while you go in and get settled? Oliva, it is a pleasure meeting you, and I know after our visit, we will become good friends. Our families have been too long parted. We need to come together and heal old wounds." Father Joseph returned to his chair on the porch. When mother withdrew her hand from her pocket, it held only a key. I smiled and nodded before heading back to Grans.

Grandma wasn't home yet, so I took it upon myself the distasteful task of wringing necks and plucking chickens. I finished just in time and could see Grandma, way down the street making her way home. That's when it struck me; I'd forgotten the rosemary. Gran was never in a hurry. I knew I could easily run home, get the rosemary, and run back before she arrived.

Mother, loving the smell of rosemary, planted ours on the side of the house right below the parlor window. Excited, I hurried stripping the rosemary from the stems until my hands were full. As I began to leave, I noticed Father Joseph was no longer on the porch. Still close to the parlor window, I stood on my tiptoes and glanced inside. What I saw sent me into a panic, and I was ready to scream when something Mother said flashed into my mind, "Survivors are those who keep their wits when all around are losing theirs."

Mamma was unconscious, bound, and gagged, hanging lifeless with her wrists tied to the banister. I could hear noises coming from her bedroom across the downstairs hall. I quickly and quietly slipped onto the front porch, slowly opening the door, slipping across the room toward Mother. As I moved, a small portion of the doorway to her room became visible through the opening into the hall. Uncle Joseph's back was to the door, and he was rifling through Mamma's dresser drawers dumping their contents onto the bed.

I could see she was breathing, but blood was trickling down her forehead from where she was struck. I started working on the ropes to free her, all the time whispering, "Mamma, wake up. Please wake up." The ropes were tight, and I was just making progress when Joseph walked into the room.

"Well, this is a fine mess. How awkward this must seem. Olivia, shouldn't you be down to yer grannies cookin' those chickens? Now I don't want you to panic, and if you help me find what I'm looking for, I'll simply go away and leave you and your mother alone. You'll never see me again. I promise," he said, in a reassuring voice.

Angry, with my heart pounding a hole through my chest, I stood firm, "If you're looking for that damn key, like my mother already told you, we don't have any key, and we don't know where the key is. Don't you think if it was here, we'd have already used it?"

"Only if you knew where to use it, and as much as I'd like to believe you, I don't so...." Pulling a knife from the back of his belt, "I'll just have to see if I can persuade you to do what's right for you and your mamma," he said, glaring at me.

I was relieved when from behind, I heard Mamma starting to come around.

Pulling a revolver from the pocket on my dress, I cocked it and pointed it directly between his eyes. "Don't take another step, or I will shoot you."

"Aw, little girl with a gun, you sure you know how to shoot that thing? Are you sure you should shoot that thing in my direction? I told you once; I get what I come for, and I'll leave. Please, you can trust me on this."

With all the threat I could muster, I glared back telling him, "Hold it right there.... I'm betting you think I'm going to lay this gun down and let you walk all over me, but I'm not the idiot child you think. I know if you got the key, you'd kill us both, and I won't let that happen. Go ahead; test my resolve, but know this, I was on the steamer Charity at the Battle of Lake and stood and watched as my mother beat your brother Felix with a shovel. Now I'm asking you once...; drop the knife and leave or take a step, and I'll put a bullet in your brain."

113

Father Joseph made his decision. I fired my revolver, and he fell to the floor. Mamma was screaming through her gag, but I couldn't take a chance. Standing over his body, I put two more bullets in his head.

Dropping the revolver, I ran to Mamma and removed her gag. As I fought to loosen the knots, she started ranting, "Oh God, what have I done? What have I done?" she cried out.

Hearing the shots, Grandma Caroline came bursting through the door. Running across the room, she helped me to release Mother from her bonds. Grabbing me tightly, Mother continued her rant. "My girl, my precious girl, what have I made you do? It's my fault; it's all my fault. I should have been there to protect you. I let this fool get the upper hand. It's my fault…. This is all my fault."

Determined, I raised my voice, "Mother I am fine, a little shaken, but I'm fine. Now stop…. Sit still so Gran and I can take care of this bleeding."

Gran nor I could believe she actually listened. Calming herself, she sat quietly, allowing us to care for her injury. Once bandaged, she came to her senses and began asking questions, difficult questions.

"Tell me again, Olivia. Are you alright or just in shock? I need to know you're alright."

"Mother, I'm fine. I remembered everything I was taught, and I followed it to the letter."

"He took my gun. How did you get my gun away from him?" she questioned.

"I didn't…. It was my gun." I dared not look at her because I knew she was giving me the same devastating gaze she gave the uncles that day on the Charity.

"Your gun…. Your gun? Where did you get your gun?" she demanded.

"Grandpa thought it would be a good idea. Uncle Hatch got me the identical gun he'd gotten for you, and Uncle Jacob taught me to shoot."

"So you lied to me; you didn't tell me you had a gun?" She challenged.

"It wasn't a lie any more than you not telling me about your gun." I justified.

"I am an adult and your mother; you don't keep secrets like this from me."

"Mamma, I know this is hard for you, and yes I am your daughter, but like it or not, I am an adult now, and I will do anything necessary to protect the people I love. I was in control the whole time."

"In control? Please tell me, if not in a rage, why an adult walked over and shot him twice more."

"It's what I was taught," I defended.

"Not by me," she said.

"No, not by you. It was Uncle Jacob. He taught me. "Once you commit, never let a good decision come back to haunt you. When faced with evil, don't shoot once and hope he's dead. Shoot until you know he's dead, and that's exactly what I did."

Neighbors hearing the shots were gathering on the front porch. Taking charge, I yelled out, "Someone get the Sheriff. There's been a killing." Mamma stared at me but didn't say a word. I could tell by her eyes that she wasn't mad at me. I think she may have just realized I was all grown up.

Grandma Caroline removed an old tablecloth from the sideboard and covered the body. I knew this wasn't over; the concerns of my mother were multiplied tenfold in the face of my Grandma Caroline. I knew Grandma was suffering, reliving that terrible night so many years ago when her gun went off killing Aldridge. She never came to terms with what she had done. Because of my actions, she now faced her worst fear, her precious granddaughter killed a man and would now be forced to share a similar guilt. In the future, I would choose my words wisely, having to feign remorse in order to ease her burden, when in truth, I felt justified. I felt no regret in what I had done.

But it was also in this moment that I began to wonder if I could have done or said anything different to have changed the outcome because even bad men have families. That's when it occurred to me, perhaps it was thoughts like these that plagued Gran's mind..., why mother became frantic when I pulled the trigger, and perhaps thoughts like these stoked the fires of Uncle Jacob's nightmares. If this is a burden of adulthood, I'd prefer to remain a child.

115

With all that blood on the floor and not knowing if he was working alone, we chose to spend the night at Grandma's house. Sitting out on her porch, she tried to find comfort and ease my guilt by reading a verse from her Bible.

"Beware of false prophets, which come to you in sheep's clothing, but inwardly they are ravening wolves." Matthew 7:15.

She was right. I did find comfort. It was as though Matthew wrote this verse just for me.

Why at night when the armor of the day falls away must conscience take hold? It is in the dark recesses of a weary mind where consequence dwells. Stealing my sleep, it burdened me with questions of why, but they were questions without answer, and so consumed in guilt, I cowered in a corner of my room and wept.

"Slipping in, Mother put her arm around me offering comfort, "Are you alright, sweetheart?" she asked.

"I'm sorry, Mamma. I didn't mean to wake you."

Stroking my hair, she assured me, "You didn't wake me."

"If I didn't wake you, why are you here?" I asked.

"Because I know you, Oliva Harris, and I have looked into the eyes of the demons that now haunt you, and I'll not let you face them alone. How about if you sleep in my room tonight, and we'll face them together?"

I am thankful for my mother.

***

Over the next few days, we began to put our lives back together. First on the list was shopping; we needed to replace the luggage and clothes that burned on the *Bertha Lee.*

Mother hired Joe Hutchinson to repair the damage to the floor. Joe said, "It'd be best to replace those bloodstained floorboards. Over the years, the finish has worn a little thin, and the blood saturated that wood."

116

She agreed, telling him, "We want no trace." She also told Joe we'd be traveling soon, and it would be a perfect time for him to recoat all the floors and make needed repairs. Mother trusted Joe, often using the word integrity to describe him to others. Joe was one of the few tradesmen where there was no discussion of price. Whatever Joe's bill, it was fair.

The family waiting in New Orleans were informed by telegraph of our situation, and letters detailing our ordeal were posted to family by mail.

Area papers reported on the killing, but it was too soon, and the body had yet to be positively identified. Mother went to the sheriff and claimed her uncle's satchel, but like the sheriff, she found no clues—just the robes and trappings of a priest.

A couple of days later, I was passing by and saw Grandma Caroline on her porch clipping newspaper articles and talking to her friends. I waved as I passed, hearing one of the ladies comment, "Poor child".

Mother penned a letter to Odila every day telling her of our journey, leaving out the bad and embellishing the good. To Mamma, Odila was a gift from God. The resurrection of this one, special, childhood friend helped ease the pain of all the others lost along the way.

Chapter XIV
The Church of Saint Augustine

It was the second week of May when we boarded a coastal steamer and headed back to New Orleans. After a couple of days with family, we were ready to investigate the next name on Carina's list—Father Giuseppe, (Joseph). It seemed redundant to me, but Mother had a suspicion about the reverend. She told me, "He may be absent, but we might still find some answers at the church. Carina scrolled beside his name, Saint Augustine Catholic Church."

Built in 1841 by free blacks and other people of good conscience, it sat on the corner of Bayou Road and Saint Claude, land formerly a part of the Claude Treme plantation estate.

The Ursuline Sisters owned the property and offered to donate the land for the building of the church with the provision the church be named after one of their patron saints, Saint Augustine. The church catered to all who entered and freely offered aid and comfort.

Two women of the church founded the Congregation of the Sisters of the Holy Family, dedicating themselves to orphaned girls, the uneducated, poor, sick, and the elderly among free people of color.

The church was instrumental in the founding of one of the first private schools for the colored. During the time of slavery, it was the most integrated congregation in the country with a congregation made up of free blacks, whites with an ethnic mix, and two outer aisles of slaves. It was a move in the right direction. It's as the Unitarian minister Theodore Parker once wrote:

"I do not pretend to understand the moral universe; the arc is a long one. My eye reaches but a little ways. I cannot calculate the curve and complete the figure by the experience of sight; I can divine it by conscience. But from what I see, I am sure it bends towards justice."

A Sister Grace greeted us at the door asking our names. Mother replied, "Pearl," pointing to herself, "and this is my daughter, Olivia."

"I'm so pleased you have come. How may I serve?" she said with a pleasant smile.

Smiling back, Mother requested, "We hoped to visit one of your priests, a Father Joseph."

"Oh, no trouble at all. Follow me; he's with the children in the churchyard."

Confused, we followed along. Stopping short, she pointed down a hall to an open door leading outside. We could hear the voices of children at play. One small girl ran into the hall, quickly slowing to a walk when she saw the Sister. "You'll find him in the yard. He'll be the man in the collar. Have a pleasant visit." We slowed as we approached the open door, allowing our eyes to adjust to the light.

Entering the yard, I suddenly felt faint. My legs gave way, and I toppled to my knees. Mother caught me in mid-fall, easing me to the ground. She couldn't help but notice the look of terror on my face. "Olivia, Olivia, what's wrong?" I began shaking violently as a priest rushed up and offered assistance. I had never been so scared, so out of control. I tried to crawl away, but Mamma was holding me. I tried to warn her but found myself mute.

"Is she alright?" the priest asked. Then he cried out, "Sisters, sisters, come and help us."

Mother started to reply, "I don't know what's wrong with—" Looking up, she stumbled back joining me on the ground. The last time we'd seen this man's face was the day I put three bullets in his head.

The Sisters tried to calm me, assuring, "There's nothing here you need to fear. It's just the Sisters and me, Father Giuseppe, and your mamma; she's right here. Please don't be afraid."

Still shaking, I looked over to Father Joseph. His eyes were trained on my mother's face and then noticing the satchel laying in the grass, he suddenly became downcast.

Let it be said, I am not easily carried away on flights of fancy. For the sake of my own salvation, I must justify the following event by believing mysterious are the ways of God. Admittedly, I cannot comprehend how at this moment I became in his mind. Filled with his sorrow, I saw the face of his brother, and although seeing Uncle Joseph remain silent, I heard him speak the name, *Stefano*. He was feeling genuine concern for mine and Mother's wellbeing. I found no evil in this man. Filled with empathy, I rose to my feet, embraced and offered comfort to my great uncle. Mother was noticeably confused.

> *I record this happening as truthful but admittedly most curious, and I cannot myself explain what it was in my mind or how it was conveyed. Please do not judge my account unworthy by this one occurrence.*

Mother was staggered by my acceptance of a man who moments ago appeared to be a horrid specter. Holding me tightly, he whispered, "I pray he didn't hurt anyone."

He led us to a private room where we could talk.

"You were a twin.... Your brother's name was Stefano, Stephen?" I asked. Mother, seemingly confounded by my assumption, sat quietly.

"Yes, what you say is true. I thank you for returning my robes. It is not the first time Stefano has taken them. You see, my brother Stephen lacked a conscience at times. He impersonated me to defraud people of their money. So how do you know Stephen?" he asked.

There was no good way to say it, so I simply stated, "He tried to kill us."

Once again deeply saddened but not surprised, he shared his feelings, "I feared it was only a matter of time. Where is he now?" he asked.

Tearing up, I confessed, "I killed your brother."

Rising, he came to me and kneeling at my feet, he took my hands and gave a most fervent prayer, absolving me of any wrongdoing and ending with, "You are but a child and blameless in your Father's eyes."

When he'd finished, Mamma held the list out, and Father Joseph immediately spoke out, "That's Carina's handwriting. How do you know Carina?" he asked. Squeezing his hands, I gazed into his eyes, and he said, "Child, you have the face of my sister Airiana. Who are you?" he asked.

"I am Olivia. Your sister Arianna was my grandmother, and this is my mother, LaRaela. She is known to most as Pearl."

"Turning his attention to Mother, he hugged her and joyfully exclaimed, "You are my niece. I know of you," he proclaimed.

"How do you know of me?" she asked.

"You can't minister to slaves without knowing their angels." He proudly stated. "This list is a list of my brothers. Felix drowned having passed over a month ago, and now you inform me Stephen is no longer with us; that leaves just me and my older brother. Why did you come here?"

Mamma explained about Carina's warning and about the search for a mysterious key and how we hoped finding the key might put an end to this insanity so my life would no longer be in peril. Still cautious, she failed to mention our entanglement with Felix or the secret of Etta and Aida, but she did voice genuine concern for the safety of Carina.

Worried, Uncle Joseph asked, "Carina, is there imminent danger?"

"We still have some time. I feel she'd be in greater danger if we rush in unprepared," she assured him.

"You're Uncle Ottaviano, and I used to visit Carina twice a week. We'd sit with her and read books and play parlor games. Ottaviano was a doting uncle engaging Carina's fancy for castles and dragons…, but after my sister Etta was murdered, her daughter Aida put a stop to our visits. For a long while, twice a week, I'd sit on the bench across the

121

street, looking over to Carina sitting in her window, and although apart, we still felt a connection.

"I have no proof it was Aida, but on my last visit, some men came out of nowhere and gave me a beating, putting me in the hospital for over a month. I feel ashamed that I am a coward and can't bring myself to go back.

"As for this key, might I offer counsel? Take my advice, and forget the key. It's a fairy tale I have endured since I was a boy. It is an apparition and will bring you only death and misery as it has to so many throughout its history.

"Now, there is a way I can assist you. If you are willing to accept an invitation to my home, you will be able to cross the last name from your list because Ottaviano, the oldest of my brothers, lives with me." Mamma hesitated, so I accepted his invitation.

Leaving the church, we spotted our driver resting with the horses in the shade of a live oak, and we signaled him to follow behind. Uncle Joseph assured us it was not so far and, "Just a good stretch of the legs."

As we walked, Uncle Joseph explained about his brother.

"Ottaviano was his Christian name, but we all called him Otto. He was the oldest brother and the best of us all. 'Smarter, strong, and better looking,' he'd often reminded us in jest. He was studying engineering wanting to be an architect; he loved to build.

"Otto served during the war and would have proudly sacrificed his life to form a Confederate states, but never having owned a slave and with many free black friends, he could not in good conscience support the institution of slavery. It was ironic that after the battle of New Orleans, it would be a scavenger, a black Union soldier to strike him in the head with the butt of a rifle and steal his life.

"Otto remembered, telling us, "He thought he'd killed me and walked over to pick my pockets, but it was I who reached out and picked his pocket, ripping it from his shirt. The fabric in Otto's hand revealed his killer—soldiers sewed their names inside clothes, allowing families to mourn and bury their dead. The pocket in Otto's hand belonged to a soldier, William Marr. Otto's wounds eventually healed, but he returned with the mind of a child."

I froze in my tracks. Looking back, Mother asked, "What's wrong?"

I repeated the name, "William Marr...," and then she understood.

Uncle Joseph asked, "Pearl, do you know this name?"

Shaking her head, she acknowledged, "If indeed it is the same man, he may well have caused injury to my family as well, but you were saying? Please continue."

"Felix and Stephen used to corrupt him and use him in their schemes, but I put a stop to them when I brought him to live with me. Treat him gently; he has a kind heart and a gentle soul.

Here we are. Please come inside, and make yourselves to home." Calling out, he announced, "Otto..., Otto, come on down. We have company. I know how much you love company. Come down, and meet your niece Pearl and her daughter Olivia. Pearl is Airiana's girl. Come down and show Olivia your major construction project." Under his breath, he confided, "He's not shy. He's more than likely tucking in his shirt tail. He won't be seen unless he's neat and tidy. Oh, and Olivia, don't be offended if he won't let you touch his project; he's very protective of his major construction project."

A voice from upstairs called down, "I'm comin', Brother Father Joseph. I just got to find my shoe."

"While we wait, let me make us some tea. I'll be right there at the kitchen counter where you can see me. Don't be scared. He is very kind."

Otto, in his late sixties, was a big man with a smile to match. You could tell by his gate, he had a slight paralysis on his left side, and as he walked, he held his left hand close to his chest. As he grew closer, you could see an indentation on the right side of his head where the butt of the rifle had struck him. I knew his condition might disturb Mother, not because she found his injury repulsive but because of the memory of Ponder in his last days.

Otto smiled, saying, "Hello Pearl." Then looking at me, he hollered out, "Brother Father Joseph, Brother Father Joseph, she looks like my sister!"

Joseph hollered back from the kitchen. "Yes she does; she's beautiful like your sister Airiana, isn't she?"

"Yeah…, beautiful like Airiana. She's like the painting. Olivia, you want to see my major construction project? I been workin' on it forever." Taking my hand, he led me into the next room. I was truly amazed when around the corner, I found myself looking at an enormous scale model of the St. Louis Cathedral, the Cathedral-Basilica of Saint Louis, King of France. The Cathedral is in New Orleans, French Quarter, and since my arrival in New Orleans, I never missed an opportunity to sit and gaze at its grandeur.

Astounded, all I could say was, "Wow."

"That's what a lot of people from the church say when they see it," he replied. "When I get tired of making the building, I make the altars and the lights and the pews and chairs. I have to go down there once in a while to make sure I paint things the right color."

"What's it made of, Uncle Otto?" I could tell right away he liked when I called him uncle.

"Well…, it's made out of sticks. Brother Father Joseph used to sit and take the fire off the end of the sticks, so they'd be safe for me to use them, but then, later on, he went down to the place they make 'em, and he bought a bunch of sticks before they put the fire on the end, so he wouldn't have to take it off again. Did I make sense?"

"You sure did, Uncle Otto. I understand perfectly well," I told him.

Excited, he asked me, "I got lots of gum all warmed up. Would you sit and put some sticks on for me?"

"Uncle Otto, I would love to help."

Uncle Joseph nearly dropped his cup when he and Mamma walked in and found me putting sticks on the Cathedral. Like me, Mother stood in awe with her mouth gaping open as she gazed upon Otto's project.

Slightly insulted, Uncle Joseph commented, "You never let me put sticks on your Cathedral."

Taunting and with a slight smirk on his face, Otto boldly stated, "It's 'cause you don't look like my sister." Otto had made a joke, and his laugh was infectious. We couldn't help but laugh ourselves, and then we couldn't stop laughing, and every time we started to calm down, Otto smiled at his Brother Father Joseph, handing me another stick, and we'd start laughing again. I can't tell you what a relief it was to finally meet relatives we liked."

We went out to eat at Otto's favorite restaurant then sat visiting late into the night. When Otto left the room to use the outhouse, Mother told Uncle Joseph she had known about Felix drowning all along but still couldn't bring herself to tell him what happened, but somehow, I think he knew.

She then brought up the subject of the painting. Uncle Joseph told us he remembered the second painting but had no idea of its whereabouts. She didn't mention Carina's story of how the key was in the first but not in the second. I think Uncle Joseph just assumed she wanted a portrait of her mother. When Otto returned, Joseph asked him, "Do you remember the big painting of Airiana?"

"Yeah, it's on the wall at the big house with all the other ancestors," Otto responded.

"What about the other one? You know, the one up in the attic."

Otto sat fidgeting, then in low voice meant only for Joseph, he told him, "I can't tell you. I made a promise. Stephen made me promise I wouldn't tell."

"Was Stephen doing something bad? Was he doing something he shouldn't have been doing? You know it wasn't his painting. What do you think Mamma would say about him making you promise?"

Thinking back Otto, studied for a moment on what Mamma had taught him. Then perking up he stated, "Brother Father Joseph, I think she'd have said," 'If a promise is based on a lie it don't count.' So I'm gonna tell ya what I know, but you ain't gonna like it."

"Why is that Otto?" Hesitating, Otto, sat staring at his brother with a most worried look on his face.

Joseph reassured him, "You know you're not going to be in trouble for telling me the truth."

Once again, in a low voice intended only for his brother, Otto whispered, "It's 'cause she's naked."

Mother and I both sat hiding a grin, still acting as if we couldn't hear the conversation.

Skeptical, Joseph pressed further. Whispering back, he asked, "How in the world did she get naked, Otto?"

Even lower, Otto whispered, "Stephen sold her to some of them men down at the Tea House. You know, the one he liked to goin' to, and it was them that painted her clothes off."

"I understand, Otto, and thank you for being so honest. Mamma would be proud of you."

"Olivia, Pearl, I think I'll let Brother Father Joseph explain to you about your painting. I think I'll go on to bed if that's all right."

Uncle Joseph assured him, "Of course you can go to bed. Goodnight Otto; have good dreams." Mother and I also wished him sweet dreams, and he headed to his room.

Mother and I sat looking to Uncle Joseph for answers, and it was with a red face Uncle Joseph began to explain. "Much as I hate to admit it, I think I understood what Otto was saying, and I am going to try to explain, but please remember, I wasn't born a priest. Growing up, my brothers and I became fascinated with a place they called the Tea House. It was a men's only Tea House. We had our suspicions, but for the most part, we'd just sit across the street watching and daring each other to run up and look through the doors.

"What fascinated us about the Tea House was the large number of men who entered but never appeared to leave. At the time, we didn't know about the exit into the alley. The main attraction for us was the fancy women coming and going. Being the youngest, to me, it seemed odd for a men's only club. Sometimes those women waved and giggled at us from across the street, and like fools, we'd wave and giggle back.

"I'd like to say it was just a lark, but one day, Felix and Stephen ran through those doors. And I tell you the truth, those same brothers who ran in that day, never really came out again. Otto tried to stop them, but they wouldn't listen. Being the youngest, Otto held me back, but I was shy, and the fact is, I'd have never left his side. I think if Otto hadn't been there, Stephen and Felix may have forced me to go with them, so in a way, Otto saved me that day, and I've found myself beholden to him ever since.

"I think you already guessed it was a brothel, but the real evil of this place was the opium den. In the beginning, they gave the opium away, but it wasn't long before Felix and Stephen were stealing to support their habits.

"Now—about the portrait—while men waited for services, these clubs kept their interest by having portraits of scantily dressed women hanging on the walls. Good portraits are expensive, and it's easier to acquire old family portraits at auction and have them touched up. I'm afraid it may be what happened to my sister's portrait.

"The good news is even though the local politicians saved their Tea House, I'm happy to report we put the opium den out of business a few years back. Chances are the portrait is still there. Your problem is they're not just going to let you and Olivia pop in for a look around, and they despise me."

Now it was Mamma's turn to have a red face, telling Uncle Joseph, "It may not be a problem. It's much to my chagrin that some of the Tea House patrons may be men in my employ."

As we pulled away, Uncle Joseph wished us safe journeys, telling us, "Don't be strangers," and Otto was waving from the upstairs window.

***

It was one o'clock in the morning when she banged on Uncle Jacob's door, telling me it was important, and he would understand. He answered the door with a sawed-off shotgun in his hand. After a brief conversation, we were back on our way to the mill.

Curious, I asked, "What did you tell Uncle Jacob? You plottin' on somebody, Mamma?

"Just relax; you'll find out in the morning," she said with a clever smile.

We slept in till seven. Then after a nice breakfast with Grandma and Grandpa, we headed back to town.

Chapter XV
Jacob's Smile

We pulled up in front of a seedy looking building. The entrance was recessed into the front like a theater; it was here two men stood like statues on either side of a French door. Some of the upstairs rooms facing the street drew attention to the building with red and pink curtains dangling out in the breeze. No need to ask. I knew from the descriptions where I was. This had to be the Tea House. As we approached the front of the building, a man burst through the door holding his hands out, and he yelled, "Woah, hold on there, ladies. Is there something we can do for you? He asked.

"No," Mamma said. "We just want to come in and look around."

"Afraid that won't be possible, sweet cheeks; ya see, this is men only, and unless you're lookin' for a job and willin' to audition for me right here on the street, you ain't comin' in. If you ain't lookin' for a job, you must be lookin' to cause trouble, and once again, you ain't comin' in. You gettin' my message, sweet cheeks? I guarantee your husband ain't in here.

You and this sumptuous child best be movin' along before you get in over your pretty, little heads." And it was in this moment, he'd found himself a little too high for his nut. Uncle Jacob and six of New Orleans' finest officers were suddenly standing right behind us.

You could have cut the tension with a knife. I looked to Uncle Jacob for strength but instead found him smiling. In all my years, I can't remember ever seeing him smile. Always restrained, you may get a grin or smirk but never a smile, and now at this most inappropriate of times, something struck him as funny, and I could only figure it was in hearing his Pearl called sweet cheeks.

Slowly losing control, he pointed to Mamma telling the man, "Sweet cheeks here has an interest in art. How about to avoid a panic among your clients, I'll have the officers stay out here, and sweet cheeks can just slip in and have a quick look around. How 'bout that?"

Realizing he was outmatched, standing before his citadel with a voice of compliance but a contrasting look of total disdain, he conceded.

"Of course, officers. We don't want any trouble. We run an honest business here. Avoid room five; the councilman doesn't appreciate interruptions." Then turning, under his breath, I heard, "Hypocrites."

Ready to burst, Jacob looked over asking, "What do you think..., sweet cheeks..., should we go inside and have a look around..., sweet cheeks?" Then winking at me, he added, "You can bring that sumptuous little daughter with ya if you don't think she'll be corrupted."

I couldn't help but be amused by his antics; even the guards by the doors were grinning. I can't imagine anyone ever calling my mother sweet cheeks without it being followed by a gunshot or a punch in the mouth, but on this rare occasion, Jacob had the upper hand.

Glaring at Jacob, I could tell she was more amazed than mad, almost cracking a smile herself. She found great pleasure in seeing him smile.

Leading us in, the proprietor asked, "Why don't you just tell me what you're looking for, so we get this over with?"

Speaking up, I began describing the painting. Impatient, he interrupted saying, "Airiana, you want to see Airiana? It's one of our most popular works," and he motioned us to follow.

It is unfortunate this place would forever be a part of my memory. In the future, if I should see something gaudy or get a whiff of rotting carcass along the road, I will think of this brothel. The men who frequent these places cannot possibly possess a sense of smell.

The portrait hung in a waiting area, and Otto was correct when he said, 'It was them that painted her clothes off,' and I must say, the artist also greatly embellished her bosoms. As I examined the painting, Mother inquired about purchasing the portrait. In the background, men negotiated price and made their choices as if selecting a prime cut from a butcher's case. The women came and went, scantily dressed. Some briefly appeared down the hallway in their altogether.

"I'll give you a hundred dollars for the painting," she told the man.

"It's our most popular piece. I can't imagine parting with it," the proprietor replied.

Annoyed and over a barrel, she threw out another offer. "A hundred and twenty-five and you supply a clean sheet, and I repeat, a clean sheet to carry it out in.

It was as he made a counteroffer, "Two hundred dollars, and the painting is yours," and then I saw it, and I couldn't believe my eyes. It's not what I expected, but it made so much sense.

Waving my hand to stop her, I called out, "Mamma, you don't need to buy it." Then smiling, I looked her in the eyes, telling her, "I know."

The proprietor, hearing my words, immediately backpedaled saying, "Well, since the painting appears to be your family, I will accept your last offer of a hundred and twenty-five, and a clean sheet it is."

"You don't need to buy the painting. I know I've found it," I told her.

"Are you certain, Olivia?"

"Trust me.... I know."

"I trust you, daughter."

Standing with me, looking up at Airiana, she told me, "My mother can't be here. I'll not leave her in this place." Turning to the proprietor, she told him, "I'll take it."

Uncle Jacob removed the portrait from the wall, and covering it in a clean sheet, we took Airiana from this place. Jacob dismissed the officer outside, sending them on their way and went to load the portrait onto the wagon.

Grabbing Mamma's arm and pulling her to a bench, I asked her for Carina's note—not the list but the original note. "You know..., the one with the name of the bank on the bottom," I told her.

As she searched for the note, I began recalling my thoughts at the time, and I told Mamma, "The paper was folded as if by a child." Finding the paper, she handed it to me, and as I unfolded, I repeated, "The paper was folded as if by a child, with many creases and in no uniform shape. The creases stained with ink." I pointed this out as I slowly unfolded, "It led to a blot that nearly obscured one of the words on the page. I felt the faded and ink-stained paper to be a reflection of Carina's state of mind.

But, Mamma, I was wrong; it's a drawing. Look at it. What we thought were stains are a rough drawing of the key."

Shocked, Mother held her hand to her chest, and I asked, "Do you have it on?" And almost in tears, she shook her head yes. "The stains in the creases are the chain, and the blot is the shape of your pearl. It's your necklace, Mamma. Your necklace is the key."

"How did you know? What did you see in the second painting?" she asked.

"Carina's words in the garden were, 'I was gazing in her eyes when I first saw it. You know their eyes don't really follow you. They're just paint. How it happened, I don't know...; the key's in the first but not in the second.' We made a mistake. The painting in the wagon is the first; the painting at the house is the second. Your grandmother must have commissioned the second painting and omitted the necklace to hide the key. Airiana, at the house, has a bare neck; Airiana, in the wagon, is wearing your necklace. Do you see? It all makes sense?"

Grabbing me by the cheeks, she kissed me on the head. "You child, are absolutely amazing. You know, you take after your mother."

We were excited and laughing when back to his old self, Jacob walked over and pointed to the wagon. "If you're done with your little party, I'm hungry, and we're ready to go."

Losing track of time, it was after one o'clock, and we had missed dinner. We each grabbed an arm and made him escort us to the wagon.

In very good humor, Mamma began patting Jacob on his belly, telling him, "How 'bout old sweet cheeks buy you some dinner?" Jacob started smiling again and helped us on the wagon.

131

Chapter XVI
Impending Doom

I woke with a sense of impending doom. Climbing out of bed, I hurried to the window. Something was wrong but impalpable. Everything seemed to be in order, but the feeling persisted. I puzzled how my eyes could deceive when this feeling was so strong. Then it occurred to me; the source of my distress was not in vision but in sound—there was none. The birds were not singing because there were no birds. The camp dogs should be scavenging the docks and chasing squirrels, but all were absent. Looking out the back window down the path was just as strange. Not one deer grazed on the woodland edge. The sky was bright but carried a yellowish, rusty tint. I dressed for breakfast hoping the morning conversation might shed some light on my feeling of dread.

As I approached the table, Uncle Hatch was reciting, "Red sky at night, sailors delight. Red sky in the morning, sailors take warning." I knew this was based on a quote from the book of Mathew. I also knew somewhere along the along way, the shepherds of the Bible must have become sailors. Seeing me approach, he squinted one eye, and in the voice of an old seafarer, he issued a warning, "Take heed shipmate. There be a storm a-brewin'. Batten down the hatches."

Curious, I asked him, "Is that why all the animals are gone?"

"It is…, and unlike people, animals sense changes and head for higher ground. Fish have a sense, and they swim to deeper water. Take it from your Uncle Hatch. I've seen this before. We're in for a gale.

Hopefully, the storm will break on the wetlands offshore and slow it down a bit before it reaches us. There's no need to worry; the house is high enough to secure us from the tides."

"How long do we have?" I asked.

"If I were to gamble a guess and she don't stall offshore, she'll hit by this afternoon."

Uncle Hatch assured me of our safety, but the nagging feeling persisted. I couldn't eat a bite. Leaving the table, I sat in the piazza looking out over the lake when suddenly I was struck by a premonition, and Carina appeared in my thoughts warning me. "Etta knows you have the key. An evil force assembles. They're coming to claim her prize." That's when I realized it wasn't the weather—Etta was the storm I feared.

Disconcerted, I tried to justify what had just happened, questioning, *Am I sick? Am I going insane? Was this a vision?* With a hand on a Bible, I would swear Carina was just standing in my mind. Her words were crystal clear, and I felt it to my very core. Carina's warning is real.

In a panic, I screamed, "Mamma," and she came running to my side, but my thoughts were confused and my words garbled at best. Frantic, I thought, *How can I explain without appearing insane?*

She looked deeply into my eyes, and she listened closely as I tried to explain. Then without question, she promptly turned announcing, "We're about to fall under attack. Captain Hatch, what are the chances we could sidestep this storm by sailing east?"

"It's hard to tell, but with the winds to the northwest, she may bounce along the coast and just graze us before she heads to Texas. If that's the case, sailing east for even a few hours, we might avoid the worst of the storm. But be advised; it would be safer to weather the storm here at the mill.

To have heard my own words, I'd have dismissed them as gibberish.

Mamma, still looking in my eyes, announced, "Pack light. We're leaving." She could tell I was relieved.

A rider was sent to inform Uncle Jacob, and within the hour, four, heavily armed wagons left the mill heading for the docks. Upon arrival, Mother and Uncle Hatch went off to arrange transport. I felt fortunate we made it this far with no signs of resistance, but now skeptical, two men in our company began spreading dissent, grumbling how their time had been better spent at the mill preparing for the storm. It had to be sheer instinct when Uncle Jacob rode up driving his horse between the two agitators, and with just a look and not a word, the rebellion was quelled.

> *As you read ahead, I ask your forgiveness, for admittedly I know little of sailing. My Uncle Hatch at times cringes at my use of nautical terms, and so it is for this reason, I apologize in advance.*

The three-masted coastal schooner *Zephyr* and crew were secured, and our own Captain Hatch Wefing was manning the helm. Two men carrying rifles in long leather cases arrived, asking for Jacob. Not long after, two men in uniform arrived with four crates on a flatbed wagon, Jacob and Grandpa supervised as the four crates marked explosive were carried aboard. Grandpa disappeared with the soldiers below deck.

Only two hours to supply and rig, and the *Zephyr* was underway tacking east along the Gulf Coast. The winds were steady at twenty-five knots. My *Zephyr* rose and fell, the water crashing onto her decks, washing from bow to stern and back to the sea. She was watertight and solid as oak.

We were an hour out when off in the distance, the smoke of a steamer was spotted on the horizon, and it appeared to be following in our wake. Apprehensive, we watched and wondered why they chose to sail on such a day.

The second hour revealed it to be a coastal sidewheel steamer, turning its back on the wind it instead relying on the powerful engines; it was quickly closing the distance. A worrisome thought now came to mind. *Was the premonition not to save but to place me in harm's way?*

Mamma and Gran were below deck, and due to circumstances beyond their control, I was in charge of myself, and I determined my place was on deck.

Off in the Distance

When one lives on the sea, one learns at an early age there are two types of people: those who have been seasick, and those who are going to be seasick. And mamma, who had never been, was now an awful shade of green. She grasped her bucket as Gran offered comfort holding a wet towel on her neck, but looking over to Gran, I could tell she wasn't far behind. The French called the sickness *Mal de mer,* and to my knowledge, it never claimed a life, although I understand those who suffer the ailment have at times considered death a viable option.

I stood in the back listening as a meeting took place below deck. My Uncle Jacob was a warrior. When it came to battle, he was no man's fool, and he spoke to rally our troops.

"Winning a battle has little to do with the size of the force and everything to do with the hearts and minds of men. Whilst appearing of little use, the rebel yell was crucial in battle, charging our troops into a frenzy and demoralizing the enemy lines. The rebel cry tested the enemies resolve, making them hesitate—the cost of hesitation being life itself.

"The legend of the 'King of Clubs' is as much fiction as fact. Cowering behind their fortification, the enemy no longer faced an army but the fear of encountering one man. Today we will take advantage of our enemies' fear and put on a show of force that will make them turn tail and run." Uncle Jacob cried out, "Prepare for battle!" And the men aboard let out the Rebel Yell. It was the sound of which I'd never heard before, and the likes of which I've never hear again. I swear, the sound curdled the blood in my veins.

After the battle on Lake Pontchartrain, word spread, and those in pursuit knew the legend and feared the King of Clubs was aboard.

With ropes, Uncle Jacob secured himself front, back, and sides to ensure he could stand tall in these rough seas. His best sharpshooter lay out of the storm, hidden on either side, commanding a clear view of the aft. The enemy steamer closed fast, the men on her deck searching for secure anchorage to free their hand so they might hold a weapon. Nearly in range, they lowered their rifles, and in a state of confusion, they stared and questioned how a man could be standing on the stern. Could it be the King of Clubs?

Uncle Jacob drew his revolvers, firing two shots at the enemy vessel. Knowing he was out of range the men on the enemy boat began taunting him from their upper deck, but a third and fourth shot struck their mark, and two of their men fell to the deck below. In disbelief, they hesitated, and that hesitation cost them another two dead. A panic set in as men scrambled for cover. The deadly aim of Uncle Jacob's sharpshooter stuffed the fear of God back into these men. The mercenaries cowering in fear just learned what the Union boys knew; "Keep your heads down men. Those southern boys are shooters."

We hoped by now they'd turn and run, but a strong commander shouting from the deck pushed them ahead. It suddenly became clear to me; we needed more drama. Dragging a piece of sailcloth, I headed for the stern. I crawled in front of Uncle Jacob, draping the sail cloth over my shoulders, and I yelled out, "Hold me up on your shoulders. Confused, but compliant, he bent over and hoisted me into the air.

Where the King of Clubs once stood, an apparition cloaked in white rose floating above the deck. Like a conductor directing an orchestra, I moved my hands and arms as though directing the waves sending them crashing down upon their decks. Men lay down their weapons and now held on for life and limb as, in their minds, the intensity of the storm suddenly increased with my appearance. Our sharpshooter kept firing, creating panic as their companions continued to fall.

Men screaming out as they ran for cover, "Witch! They brought an Agnusdei witch. She'll drown us all." It didn't matter if not all believed. I needed just enough for a mutiny.

Fighting the waves, two men on her bow succeeded in loading the cannon and were ready to fire when the first of two oddities occurred. Frightened and fearing the worst, I reached high and was gazing into the heart of the storm when my fingers began to burn as if pricked by a hundred pins, and when I cast my arms down, a bright flash of lightning struck their bow. The men manning the cannon were nowhere to be seen. Those who stood in witness ran to seize the wheel and turn the ship.

The vessel turned but not fast enough. Throwing my arms to the oncoming storm, I held out my hands as if to summon a wave, but as if weighted, I struggled to lift my arms, and to my wonder, as I slowly raised my hands, a great wave also rose, striking the steamer's starboard side, capsizing her into the sea.

***

I record these oddities as truthful, but admittedly most fortuitous, and cannot myself hope to explain. Please do not discount the ends by questioning of the means, for in my mind, I also try and reconcile these oddities as happenstance. Perhaps the weight I felt in my arm was from the wet sailcloth?

The cheer was short lived as the bow of our schooner rose climbing the rogue wave. Grabbing me, Uncle Jacob wrapped me in canvas, holding me fast to the deck. The crest was only half the peril marked as the bow dropped and the stern heaved to the sky. Near vertical, we plummeted down our bow driving deep into the sea and rising just in time to slice the next wave. We survived, and quickly coming about, put the sea at our stern riding the waves to harbor.

The storm had passed by the time we anchored. The dock lay in ruin, and the shoreline was flooded. Uncle Hatch yelled out to Uncle Jacob, "You're welcome."

Uncle Jacob responded back with, "For what?"

"For winning the battle and making you look good in the process," he boasted.

Shaking his head in disbelief, Jacob asked, "How on God's green earth do you figure that?"

"I figure it correctly because if I'd been you at this helm, we'd all be dead right now."

Scoffing, Uncle Jacob picked up a piece of debris and hurled it at Hatch's head. Easily dodging the projectile, Hatch ignored Jacob and gave me a little wave. Jacob turned and walked away, and Hatch began to smile.

Hatch stayed aboard, and I caught a ride to shore with Jacob and his sharpshooter. As we rowed to shore, Uncle Jacob gave me a salute, "Good work soldier. Your quick thinking is what saved our necks."

Looking back at the *Zephyr*, I saw Grandpa and the two men in uniform stacking those crates on deck. "What's in those crates Uncle Jacob?"

"Those were our last line of defense, four naval mines. If the enemy got too close, Michael and the soldiers stood ready to deploy them in our wake and blow those bastards sky high. Don't tell your Uncle Hatch, but they're on loan from our friend, the naval commander."

Thinking I understood, I concluded, "So that was the explosion on the bow of the steamer…? It was a mine?"

"No. We didn't use the mines. I don't know how you did it girl, but that lightning bolt was all yours."

Zephyr, at rest.

As Jacob and I landed, two of our horses saw us and wandered over, still pulling a camp wagon. We were concerned and hopeful the driver survived, and if so, we hoped he had a good excuse why the horses were left to wander.

Mother arrived with Gran on the next boat. Even with water up to her knees, I could tell she was glad to be back on land, but before she reached the dock, one of the camp workers rode up handing her an envelope. I looked on from over her shoulder. It was an urgent request from Cyrus.

He wrote:

> *"Pearl, come with the greatest of speed.*
> *"I fear all is lost. Miss Carina has suffered an episode the likes of which I've never seen. Yesterday at one, out of her mind, she began flailing around the parlor singing out, 'She's found the key; the key is found. She's*

found the key; the key is found. Then screaming toward the stairs at the top of her lungs, 'It's time to go to Hell, Etta. It's time to go to Hell.' I could not calm her. She ranted for an hour before collapsing.

"She's asking for her Pearl; I believe she speaks of you. I can hear Etta rampaging upstairs. She's breaking everything. I write in haste. I'll do my best to blockade these doors. Miss Carina is in danger. I implore you; please, come to her aid."

Speaking my thoughts aloud, "We were in the Tea House at one o'clock; how could Carina know we found the key?"

Without a word, mother climbed on to the wagon seat, took the reins, and cried out, "Ya! Ya!" I barely made it onto the back of the wagon as it pulled away.

"Where we goin'?" I cried out.

"We have to get to Carina before it's too late."

There was water everywhere. Over two feet of rain had fallen, but as Hatch predicted, the storm ran the coast offshore heading for Texas, and with no rain to the north to swell the rivers, the water was already receding. The streets were a maze of debris slowing our progress, but undeterred, she willed the team ahead.

Arriving at the townhouse, we burst through the doors onto a horrific and most unexpected sight. Uncle Joseph, nursing an injured leg, sat propped against the wall at the base of the stairs.

Upon seeing us, he cried out, "It's Etta! Etta's alive! She shot me, Pearl." Pointing across the hall to the parlor, "Help Otto! Someone was moaning. I sent him to check."

Mother attended to Joseph's wound, and I checked on Otto. Glancing in the parlor, I saw Otto was helping Cyrus into a chair.

"Hello, Olivia. He got hit on the head, and I'm helping him," explained Otto.

"Thank you, Otto. You stay here, and watch out after Cyrus and your brother," I told him. "Otto, do you know where Etta and Carina went? Did you see them, Otto?

Coming around, Cyrus pointed up, "Etta's on the third floor. Please hurry; she has Carina."

Having bound Joseph's wound, Mother was already hurrying up the stairs with me in pursuit. As we ran, she pulled the necklace over her head, gripping it in her hand.

A short hall on the third floor led to the open door of a darkened room. The rooms only light passed in from the hall door, and the dim light of the rising moon shone through open balcony doors on the far wall.

Mother cried out, "Etta it's me, Pearl. I have your key right here in my hand. Give me Carina, and you can have the key."

Not knowing what to expect, I stopped just short of the doorway, securing a brass hall tree to use as a weapon. Mamma had no more entered the room than she was ambushed and knocked to the floor. Etta struck at her wrist with a fire poker, and breaking Mother's grip, she seized the necklace. But before she could inflict another blow, I swung the heavy base of the hall tree. Catching her in the chest, she toppled to the floor. I helped Mother to her feet as Etta scrambled across the room to a chair where Carina sat bound. Retrieving a saber from beneath the chair, she held the blade to Carina's throat.

"Stop Etta! You have the key, Etta! Let Carina go, and we'll leave. I swear; you'll never see us again," she promised.

Out of her mind, she screamed, "No! This retched child has been a thorn in my side since the day she was born, and I will see to it she joins her worthless sister." Suddenly realizing she had nothing to barter, she stilled herself. "But perhaps I am too hasty. Pearl, if you and your little bitch will take leave of this place, as soon as I am safely away, I will release her. Otherwise, I will hack her to bits right here in front of your eyes, and then I'll come for your daughter."

With all my senses, I focused on her eyes, just as Uncle Jacob had taught me. I watched for any sign of hesitation, and that's when I'd attack and put an end to her.

All it took were the balcony doors banging in the wind. The second she turned, I charged. Catching her dress on the coat hooks, I pushed with all my might. Panicked, Etta hacked at the brass bar with her saber. Mother and Joseph ran in behind me to free Carina.

The hooks held fast in the fabric, and the saber had little effect on the heavy, brass shaft. "Free Carina, and run," I yelled.

Once freed, instead of escaping, Carina disappeared into the darkness, quickly returning with an Italian flag. *Worthless* I thought..., until the moment the brass spire on the tip pierced Etta's side. Etta screamed out. Wrenching in pain, she relentlessly continued to hack at us with the saber, but now, each time the saber fell, Carina pushed harder driving the spire deeper between her ribs, lessening the power of her blows.

Picking up speed, we forced Etta toward the balcony. Faster and faster we pushed until, off balanced, she stumbled on the threshold, falling out against the rail. Rusted bolts in wet mortar couldn't take the strain, and with Etta aboard, the top of the rail fell away from the house.

Clambering, she tried to gain purchase on the rail, the angle worsening as the iron center posts continued bending beneath her weight.

Then unforeseen, Carina dropped her pole and leaping from the balcony threw herself on Etta. The old iron posts bending over double snapped in two, and Carina and Etta fell from view.

Dumbfounded, I stood staring toward the moon. Mother, nursing a broken wrist, joined me, and we carefully moved to the edge. Peering over, expecting the worst, it was to our joy and amazement we looked into Carina's face. She clung to a piece of rail hooked over the tip of a stone corbel. Reaching over, I grabbed her wrist, trying to pull her hand higher, so she might find a more secure hold. Then miraculously, I heard a welcomed voice, "Hello Carina. What you doin' down there? Olivia, let me help you." Otto stooped down beside me and taking Carina by the hands pulled her to safety.

Safe on the balcony, Carina held his cheeks and told him, "You have always been and will always be a noble knight of this house, and I just knew it would be my noble knight, Otto, to come to my rescue."

Blushing, Otto replied, "Aw, cut it out, Carina. All I did was pull you up. Carina, I got to go back downstairs and take care of Brother Father Joseph and Mr. Cyrus."

Back inside, Carina collapsed on the couch and called out, "Pearl, Olivia, please, come and sit. I promise to behave. Once we'd settled in, Carina continued, "Did you know Etta employed Cyrus to inform on me? She never thought it possible anyone could ever care for me, but Cyrus did, and over time, he has become like a father…. He would die for me.

I'm afraid what you see tonight is the best I have to offer. Cyrus would call this one of my lucid moments…, even though what I have to say will make you question?

These days it's hard for me to distinguish between the two of me. My visions come shattered like glass, and the message to me is opaque, such as the time when Pearl's great beast fell upon an *Albany*. I could not hope to understand why, but I feared for your life; perhaps it makes some sense to you." Whereas Carina vision was incomplete, sensing only a faceless, great beast and the name of a city. Mamma and I both understood the *Albany* was the derelict steamer where she stayed as a girl, and the great beast had to be Hickory exploding from the water and crushing Pearl's murderous assailant into the *Albany*'s deck.

Albany

Angry and concerned, I interrupted, "Carina what in the world possessed you to commit suicide and jump from the balcony?" I scolded. "You scared me half to death."

Very excited, she responded, "My visions have been very dark of late, but today at the height of the storm, I envisioned all of us having a

144

picnic with someone called Iola, but I never saw her face, and I knew it was not my time to die because I have not yet met Iola."

Astounded by her answer, we sat speechless as she continued.

"I've been inflicted with the sight from the day of my birth, but, Olivia, the likes of you has not been seen for millennia. I have no proof of my claim but to speak of a clouded vision of you commanding a bright light and raising the sea. It makes no sense to me, but I saw it none the less.

I can help you avoid my mistakes. You mustn't hide your light. It is not evil but good you will seek. I see your purpose as it comes clear to you, and the children in this world will benefit.

Pearl, at times even you have questioned the existence of an unseen force shielding the Agnusdei family. You have found a great purpose in your life, but you do not carry the gift. The true purpose of your life sits before you." And she pointed to me. "She has always been with you. She was not conscious of this world and only a twinkle in your eye, but she was the driving force of your intuition, protecting you from harm.

"He was your father Pearl, but you called him Dray; for the same reason, I called her Etta, not Mother. We both had an unworthy parent. The downfall of our family was foreseen three generations back, and the identity of the key was hidden to all but a few. Grandma Airiana knew but did not share it with Etta and died before she could safely give it to you.

"In my life, it has never been a choice of good or bad but rather to choose the lesser of evils. The family fortune dwindling, Etta and Aida began selling off any excess to allow them to maintain the appearance of wealth, all the time searching for the key.

"I sided with Aida, the lesser of my evils. Taking credit for my abilities she used my visions to win the support of the remaining families, infuriating Etta. Aida's greed and ambition soon consumed any spark of good remaining. If not for their outward appearance, it was hard for me to tell them apart.

"I started to hide my visions from Aida, and she claimed it was my own fault when she felt the need to employ her little tortures upon me."

With concern, I asked, "She tortured you? What did she do to you, Carina?"

"I was never strong like cousin Pearl. My threshold of pain is low. Sewing needles and hot candle wax were usually enough, but things escalated dramatically from there. Someday I'll show you my scars and burns.

"Forgive me for saying, but the visions continue as I speak. Please take no alarm or think me cruel when I tell you, Etta lives. Water broke her fall, and she survives but is of no threat to us. Her life fades quickly. She will not last this hour, and yet, in knowing my soul revels as she falls into darkness, I feel a great burden is lifting."

Sliding from the couch, Carina knelt and held Mamma's hand. We both gasped when from her other hand, she released her grip, and the necklace dangled down. Holding it over Mamma's hand, she lowered it into her palm. "I had to get it. Etta would have destroyed it before she'd let it fall to someone else. Now you know why I jumped. Put an end to this, Pearl. Claim the treasure, and put an end to this once and for all."

Chapter XVII
Back in Harm's Way

Upon waking the next morning, the first thing Carina and I did was open the drapes, and after some judicious tapping with a hammer, we opened some windows as well. By mid-morning, our family all gathered at the Agnusdei house for introductions, and I'd have to say we were looking a little worse for wear—Cyrus with a bandage on his head. My Uncle, Father Joseph, all stitched up with a wrapping on his leg; Mamma's wrist in a splint.

Feeling a little left out, I decided then and there to show them my prize. With both hands, I pulled my dress open just far enough to reveal a long scar on my right side just above my waist. Proud as a peacock, I smiled at Uncle Jacob and told him, "It's where the bullet grazed me on the *Zephyr*." And then boastfully, I bragged, "It went through the meat but didn't' even touch the bone. It's my first gunshot wound Uncle Jacob."

The room behind me became deathly quiet, and suddenly I realized what I had done. With a bewildered look, Jacob stared at me, refusing to look at Mother. I watched in terror as the color left his face, and that's when I felt it. It was as if her eyes were burning a hole in the back of my neck. Holding my hand to my mouth, all I could utter was, "Sorry Uncle Jacob." But it was too late to shut the doors; the horse had already bolted. Even though I knew they wouldn't stay mad for long, I was feeling bad for pulling Jacob down with me and putting him back in harm's way.

Later in the morning, Mother asked me about something Carina said. "What did she mean, 'I see your purpose as it comes clear to you, and the children in this world will benefit.' I didn't understand. Did it make sense to you?" she asked.

"Mamma, you know I support our cause against slavery, but it's no longer about north and south. This new form of slavery grips the nation as a whole. Commerce follows no maps, and these men of commerce, these industrialists from both north and south seek to exploit the blacks of the south to increase their profits.

"Convict leasing is legal in the south, and the problem, as I see it, is many of the men exploiting prison laborers are also some of the same men who occupy the seats of government. We can no longer just buy freedom. Slavery today is condoned by the courts, and if we're to lease and liberate in the eyes of the law, we become the criminals. We must change the laws. We must seed our courts and government with men of good conscience. We must change the hearts of men. The battle we fight today against peonage and convict leasing has to be waged in the courts and the hall of government, and you know I will never give up the fight.

"But it's when I think of little Pearl, homeless, wandering the streets, I find my tears. Mamma, in this city, we frequent the paths of great wealth and marvel before the temples, ignoring the multitude of paths leading to its poverty. Children rummage through rubbish for meals. Homeless sleep like animals having to seek out any refuge, falling asleep with no assurance of wakening. My greatest nightmares are of children being subjugated by the dregs of this world, people the likes of Dray and Etta, who take from these children all that is good and then cast them aside.

"It has become like a thorn stuck in my mind It is an image haunting my dreams. I need to help these children and not just here but everywhere. I need to make them safe. I need to feed them, clothe them. I need to educate them so this poverty can be stopped. I can no longer allow it to run rampant and unchecked."

"There is no holding you back, and I will no longer try. In you, I see myself. The overwhelming passion you feel is the same passion driving me. You have an understanding beyond your years, and I have never been so proud," said Mother.

"We will claim whatever this key opens, and we will put our lives back in order. Then we will seek out people of like minds and make a plan, your plan, and you will be the heart and soul of your own movement, and I am certain the children will benefit."

***

The flooding along the coast took a terrible toll, but in the weeks to follow, cholera claimed the greater numbers. The storm continued on to Texas where the town of Indianola was laid to waste, never to recover.

A disgrace to the family and unwilling in life to claim her own name, Etta's body was buried in a common grave…, her testament recorded in the family Bible as simply deceased.

Overnight, Carina's mind became passive, and her visions all but ceased. Perhaps being surrounded by loving family was the distraction she needed to begin building a new life. Someday soon, on one of her future visits to Apalachicola, we would have to introduce her to Iola in person.

Mamma contacted the bank, and they made all the arrangements. Traveling to New York City our first stop was Black, Starr & Frost jewelers for verification of the key. We watched as skillful hands removed the pearl. On the top of the pearl, beneath the mount, appeared an engraving of the Agnusdei crest. Several numbers were then taken from beneath the mount itself. A letter of verification was written and placed in the hand of a Pinkerton who immediately left for the bank.

We made our way to the carriage and headed for our meeting with the banker from the *Banca Monte dei Paschi di Siena*, but when we arrived at the agreed address, Fifth Avenue from 46th to 47th Streets, instead of a bank, we were received into the lavishly appointed lobby of the Windsor Hotel.

We thought ourselves savvy in the ways of banking but suddenly found ourselves overwhelmed, as we were received by not one but at least ten bankers, all lined up in a row assembled for no reason but to greet us. Two floors of suites and meeting rooms were reserved for just our visit.

Escorted to a conference room, we were seated at a spectacular marble table with a wooden border and elaborately carved wooden legs.

With the verification in hand, a spokesman for the bank expressed gratitude to their oldest and most valued client the Agnusdei family for entrusting *Banca Monte dei Paschi di Siena* with their investments over the centuries. Also, they expressed their sincere hope we might allow them to continue investing our funds, assuring us of even greater prosperity.

Mother inquired, "Having just taken charge of the account, I am at a disadvantage; can you tell me how much is in the account?"

Caught off guard, one of the gentlemen responded, "We don't really know at this time. You see, it's invested all over the world. Given time, perhaps a few months, we should be able to give you an estimate. But please note—"

Impatient, another gentleman with a Boston accent interrupted, responding, "Mrs. Agnusdei Kohler Harris, Miss Agnusdei Harris, if I might intercede on behalf of my colleague...." His colleague gladly yielding the floor. "You have expressed you are unfamiliar with these accounts, and it is my belief you may be viewing your accounts in the wrong context. I think you came today expecting more of a common bank account, an account showing a balance at the bottom of a ledger sheet. When in reality, it may be better and more accurate to think in terms of a small country."

"A small country?" Mother puzzled.

"Yes..., indeed, a small country. The work required to reduce your accounts to a single dollar value is similar to the work needed in calculating a selling price for Italy. But allow me to assure you, in the final accounting, it is plausible to assume you would have more than sufficient funds to make the purchase."

I sat, doing my best to maintain some modicum of composure, excited at the prospect of boundless money to finance my own new purpose. It was all I could do to keep from erupting in celebration.

Mamma's reaction seemed to the contrary. I worried she may be coming ill. Looking very pale, she simply responded, "Oh dear Lord, not again."

The End

Postscript

Although I stand witness to the accounts held in these pages, I also know some incidents appear outlandish. I record these incidents as factual but can offer no explanation, for they lie beyond my sphere of understanding. No one doubts more than I, in hearing claims of sight beyond the present, but Carina has made me question my arrogance in knowing the mind of God.

In the future, I will live my life open to all possibilities, discounting none. Using any means, acquired or inherent, I will strive to fulfill my purpose.

I am Olivia Agnusdei Harris and it is now I who ask you to forgive me my visions, for they appear as shattered glass and are obscure to me, but I sense that someday when the world is more accepting, a ranger will come to record these accounts and may better explain these happenings.

So I say to the Agnusdei women who follow in my footsteps, you can expect a visitor.

Olivia Agnusdei Harris. September 20th, 1886

References

Willoughby, Lynn. Fair to Middlin': The Antebellum Cotton Trade of the Apalachicola / Chattahoochee River Valley. University of Alabama Press, Tuscaloosa, Alabama. 1993.

Zinn, Howard. A People's History of the United States: 1492 to Present. Harper Perennial Modern Classics. New York. 2005.

Smith, Julia Floyd. Slavery and Plantation Growth in Antebellum Florida 1821 —1860. University Press of Florida. Gainesville, Florida. 1973.

Rogers, William Warren. Outposts on the Gulf: Saint George Island & Apalachicola from Early Exploration to World War II. University of West Florida Press. Pensacola, Florida. 1986

Mueller, Edward A. Perilous Journeys: A History of Steamboating on the Chattahoochee, Apalachicola, and Flint Rivers, 1828 — 1928. Historic Chattahoochee. 1990.

Turner, Maxine. "Naval Operations on the Apalachicola and Chattahoochee Rivers 1861 — 1865." Alabama Historical Quarterly. 1975.

Rose, P.K. "The Civil War: Black American Contributions to Union Intelligence." CIA Center for the Study of Intelligence. U.S. Government. Washington. D.C. 2007.

Orman family, for archive materials.

Owens, Harry P. "Apalachicola Before 1861." Florida State University, Ph.D. Dissertation. University Microfilms, Inc., Ann Arbor, Michigan. 1966. (Thank You, Harry)

John Milton to Col. W. J. Magill, Feb. 20, 1864. Milton Letterbook, 44, Florida State Archives, Tallahassee. OR Union and Confederate Navies in the War of the Rebellion, Series I, Vol. 17, 350.

Blackmon, Douglas A.. Slavery by another Name: (The re-enslavement of black Americas from the Civil War to World War II). Publisher Anchor.

The city of Apalachicola, Florida, and the wonderful people who cherish and preserve its history.

Photo Credits

Credit for the following photos to the State Archives of Florida "Florida Memory Project:

DG01370 Close-up view of a sailing ship on the Apalachicola Bay. 1899. Black & white digital image, State Archives of Florida, Florida Memory. <https://www.floridamemory.com/items/show/259514>, accessed 11 December 2017.

N033317 King, Joseph W. Bank, and J.E. Grady & Co. - Apalachicola, Florida. 188-. Black & white photo negative, 4 x 5 in. State Archives of Florida, Florida Memory. <https://www.floridamemory.com/items/show/142741>, accessed 11 December 2017.

PR00290 Ruge Brothers Packing Company - Apalachicola, Florida. 1895. Black & white photo print, 8 x 10 in. State Archives of Florida, Florida Memory. <https://www.floridamemory.com/items/show/280>, accessed 11 December 2017.

PR02828 Tole's Hotel Drayton Island, Florida. 188-. Black & white photo negative, 8 x 10 in. State Archives of Florida, Florida Memory. <https://www.floridamemory.com/items/show/2675>, accessed 11 December 2017.

PR09999 Paddle steamboat. 19--? Black & white photograph, 8 x 10 in. State Archives of Florida, Florida Memory. <https://www.floridamemory.com/items/show/8454>, accessed 11 December 2017.

RC03530 Sternwheel steamer "Naiad". 18--? Black & white photo print, 8 x 10 in. State Archives of Florida, Florida Memory.

<https://www.floridamemory.com/items/show/27144>, accessed 11 December 2017.

RC06391 Skerrett, R. G. Watercolor of Confederate steamer "Planter". 1901. Black & white photo print, 10 x 6 in. State Archives of Florida, Florida Memory.
<https://www.floridamemory.com/items/show/29639>, accessed 11 December 2017.

St. Charles Hotel, New Orleans

Orman Family Archive. Orman House.

About the Author

After a working career and raising two daughters, my wife and I moved to the Florida Panhandle. It was in the historic town of Apalachicola that I began creating and caring for the Orman House State Park Museum. When I started, the house was an empty shell. Immersed in local history, I now enjoy sharing Apalachicola's rich heritage with thousands of visitors from around the world. Apalachicola Pearl, Apalachicola Gold, and Apalachicola Mother of Pearl were born from my passion for the town's history and its people. My sincere wish is for you to enjoy reading the books as much as I enjoyed writing them.

www.ingramcontent.com/pod-product-compliance
Lightning Source LLC
Chambersburg PA
CBHW030511260626
47157CB00005B/1736